# Her lips were parted, throbbing with feeling

When Julian ended the kiss and held Berry at arm's length, she stared up at him with wild eyes.

"What on earth's the matter?" he asked impatiently. "Are you a man hater or something? Have you had a bad love affair that's made you decide to dispense with men?"

"If I've decided to dispense with men, it's got nothing to do with you!" Berry snapped, then wrenched herself free and ran upstairs to her flat.

Long after his car had roared away, Berry was still trembling with reaction. Julian didn't know how close he'd come to guessing her problem. And now, out of the blue, just when she was regaining her lost confidence, this arrogant, dictatorial senior consultant had crashed through the barrier she'd so carefully constructed....

**Sue Peters** grew up in the idyllic countryside of Warwickshire, England, and began writing romance novels quite by chance. "Have a go," her mother suggested when a national writing contest sponsored by Mills and Boon appeared in the local newspaper. Sue's entry placed second, and a career was born. After completing her first romance novel, she missed the characters so much she started another and another.... Now she's as addicted to writing as she is to gardening, which she often does as she's formulating new plots.

## Books by Sue Peters

HARLEQUIN ROMANCE

1975—CLOUDED WATERS
2030—ONE SPECIAL ROSE
2104—PORTRAIT OF PARADISE
2156—LURE OF THE FALCON
2204—ENTRANCE TO THE HARBOUR
2351—SHADOW OF AN EAGLE
2368—CLAWS OF A WILDCAT
2410—MARRIAGE IN HASTE
2423—TUG OF WAR
2471—DANGEROUS RAPTURE
2501—MAN OF TEAK
2583—LIGHTNING STRIKES TWICE
2812—NEVER TOUCH A TIGER
2892—ENTRANCE TO EDEN
2915—CAPTURE A NIGHTINGALE

# One-Woman Man

## Sue Peters

# Harlequin Books

TORONTO • NEW YORK • LONDON
AMSTERDAM • PARIS • SYDNEY • HAMBURG
STOCKHOLM • ATHENS • TOKYO • MILAN

Original hardcover edition published in 1988
by Mills & Boon Limited

ISBN 0-373-02938-1

Harlequin Romance first edition October 1988

# CHAPTER ONE

THE face was contorted. Tormented. It stared at her whitely from out of the shadows.

The shock of it rooted Berry's feet to the aisle of the small hospital chapel, as the man turned in his seat and looked up, full into her face.

She had not seen him there when she entered the building. She was intent upon replacing the hassock she had mended after last Sunday's service, and getting back to the warmth of the studio as quickly as possible.

In her haste, her toe caught against a wilting flower arrangement, still waiting to be removed after the harvest festival service. It scraped noisily on the stone floor, and instantly the stranger lifted his face from his hands, and turned.

Startled into immobility, Berry stared back.

At this time in the evening, she had not expected to find anyone in the chapel. Uneasily, she was conscious of the isolation of the small building from the main part of the hospital, of the spacious tarmac car park between them, and it seemed to emphasise the silence, making the guttering candles a faint whisper in her straining ears.

Their light threw the man's face into sharp relief. It was a strong face, hewn in sharp planes, with the skin stretched tightly—too tightly—over a determined jawline.

The face was twisted with an unspeakable agony.

'I—I'm sorry,' Berry blurted out, not knowing why

5

she should apologise, since she had as much right here as the stranger. Heartily she wished she were somewhere else. She felt deeply shocked by the depths of pain in the finely drawn features confronting her, and not a little nervous to find herself alone with the stranger in this isolated spot.

'I was just bringing this hassock back. I'll drop it somewhere and go,' she mumbled.

Hastily, she dropped it beside the wilting flower arrangement. Whoever came to take the flowers away would see the hassock there, and put it back in its rightful place under one of the seats.

Berry felt incapable of moving among the seats herself to replace it. To do so, she would have to pass the stranger, who was slowly rising to his full and not inconsiderable height.

She turned hurriedly to make an exit, but before she had taken two steps the man was beside her. She jerked to a halt, and found herself staring up into eyes of a clear, bright green. Cat's eyes, spaced wide under a high forehead, surmounted by dark auburn hair.

It was tousled, as if he had been running desperate fingers through its thick waves, but in the few seconds that it had taken him to reach her he had brought his expression under control.

It was as if he had pulled down a mask, erasing all feeling except from his eyes. Not even the sternest will-power was capable of entirely masking the eyes. Only closed lids were of any real use for that purpose.

In place of the torment was a cold, hard, repelling look, that rejected the compassion that must surely show on her face, and it left Berry in no doubt that the man bitterly resented her being a witness to his private, vulnerable moment.

From the stern cast of his features, she guessed that such moments would rarely, if ever, be on display to another.

He regarded Berry from what she judged must be well over six feet, to her own modest five feet two, and her earlier unease at the isolation of the chapel returned in a rush.

The silence in the little building at this late hour was absolute and, when the stranger spoke, Berry jumped violently, betraying her nervousness.

'I suggest you put the hassock back where it belongs.' His curt tone turned his suggestion into an order. 'If you leave it there, someone's bound to trip over the thing, and give the hospital another customer. That's the last thing we want, with the wards full to overflowing already, and the staff stretched to their limit.'

The last thing *we* want . . .

That pointed to the man belonging to the hospital, although in what capacity Berry was unable to guess. The faultless cut of his dark grey suit, and the silk shirt and tie, suggested seniority.

Perhaps he was a consultant? Berry wrinkled her brows, trying without success to recall if she had ever seen him before. His was not a face that she would be likely to forget but, since she timed her visits to the wards to avoid the doctors' rounds, it was possible to go for a considerable period of time, in a place the size of St Luke's without bumping into any one particular person.

From his dictatorial manner, Berry deduced the man must think himself to be a very particular person indeed, and expect others instantly to recognise his superiority, and her hackles rose as her sympathy waned.

These days she was not inclined to obey anybody's orders meekly, particularly those issuing from an arrogant stranger, but something in the piercing quality of those green eyes compelled her and, without quite knowing how, she found her feet walking her towards the chair she had occupied on Sunday.

Angry with herself as well as with the stranger, she bent and dumped the hassock in place, and hoped when she straightened up that he would be gone. To her consternation, when she turned to go back, he was still standing where she had left him, watching her, and waiting in silence for her to rejoin him.

Unnerving silence. Berry was edgily conscious of each step she took. The man watched her walk along the aisle with the same close concentration with which her gym mistress used to watch her during deportment lessons!

An urge to giggle rose in Berry's throat. She could almost hear Miss Thompson's shrill voice calling, 'Backs straight, girls. Heads up.'

Her own unconsciously straightened as she reached him, and he turned beside her and said, 'I'll take you back to the main block.'

Telling her, not asking her, Berry realised with an uprush of irritation, and retorted, 'I can take myself. I know the way.'

'That's beside the point. In case you hadn't noticed, casualty has got the usual bunch of rowdies milling about by the entrance.'

The contempt in his tone stung like a whiplash, but whether it was directed at her own lack of observation, or at the unruly behaviour of the small crowd of youths by the casualty doors, it was difficult to tell.

Berry rejected its application to herself with a proud lift of her chin, but she could not help a sneaking feeling of relief that she had the tall, forbidding figure beside her as they approached the group.

The revellers staggered and catcalled, and Berry felt a hand cross her back and descend on her shoulder, drawing her close to its owner's side.

Doubtless, if she had not been shrouded in her borrowed hospital cloak, he would have taken her by the arm instead, in the approved manner, but nevertheless the unexpected familiarity took her by surprise, and raised her eyes in startled questioning to his face.

His hand seemed to burn through the thick woollen stuff of the cloak, and she tried to pull herself free from the sensation. It was unaccountably disturbing, far more so than the rowdy revellers. Feeling her instinctive shrug to remove his hand, the stranger's grip tightened, obliging her to remain beside him as they passed through the small crowd.

His look silenced any bawdy overtures they might have made in Berry's direction, and the youths parted sheepishly to allow them access to the swing doors of casualty, and on to the lifts in the corridor beyond.

Immediately they were inside, the stranger's hand dropped from her shoulder to his side, but the imprint of his fingers seemed to linger like five burning spots as Berry walked with him towards the lifts.

'Which department do you belong to, Sister?' he enquired, his finger poised above the lift button.

'Sister? Oh, I see what you mean.' The reason for his mistake dawned upon Berry. 'I'm not a sister. This cloak I'm wearing isn't mine. I borrowed it from Trish Connelly on surgical, just to cross the car park in. I came out without my coat, and she said it had gone cold outside.'

'Then who . . .?' Green eyes raked over Berry alertly, questioning the presence of an unauthorised outsider in the hospital at night, moreover, one masquerading in a hospital cloak.

'I'm Berry Baker, from the hospital radio. You must have heard our broadcasts.'

'I haven't got the time to listen to radio programmes.'

His tone and his look trivialised her work, and Berry flushed angrily, but before she had time to retort he went on,

'Surgical's on the ground floor, so you won't need the lift to return your borrowed plumes.'

A long finger selected one of the lift buttons, so quickly that Berry had no time to notice which one, and the decisive jab brought the cage humming down to the caller's bidding.

It would not dare to do anything else for this man, Berry decided, remembering the umpteen times she had pressed the buttons herself, and watched with mounting frustration as the lift zoomed in the opposite direction from the one in which she wanted to go, until in desperation she gave up, and flogged herself up endless flights of stairs in order to get round the wards in time before the evening broadcast.

The gates clanged shut on the man's taut nod, and the last Berry saw of her escort was a pair of dark grey, trousered legs and highly polished shoes that, from her brief glimpse of them, she suspected were handmade, disappearing up to one of the floors above.

Upstairs, she remembered belatedly, was where the senior St Luke's consultants had their own rooms. Only those of the lesser fry were designated as offices.

The stranger's face seemed to pursue her as she hooked the borrowed cloak back on to its peg in Trish's ward office and accepted the sister's invitation to, 'Come in for a coffee as usual, after you close down tonight?'

'Thanks, I'll do that. It'll be later tonight, though. We've got the mayor in for a question-and-answer session, and it always runs over its time when he's here. I'll need a coffee afterwards, I'm bound to feel parched.'

'You shouldn't talk so much.'

'I wouldn't be of much use as a broadcaster if I didn't, would I?'

With this parting shot, Berry ran upstairs to the studio, where true to her prediction she found the question-and-answer session was still in full swing. It went on for another half-hour before John Barclay, her producer and fellow announcer, called a halt, and handed Berry the microphone as usual, to close down the programme for that night.

Thrusting aside all thoughts of her encounter with the stranger in the chapel, Berry swung into the familiar routine.

'This is Berry Baker, saying goodnight, everybody. From me, and from all of us at the St Luke's Hospital Radio Broadcasting Studio. Goodnight, everybody.'

Her cheerful voice rang through the closed-circuit broadcasting system and brought smiles to many of the faces of the patients, who felt a genuine regret that the programme was over for another evening.

'I shall miss that lass when I goes 'ome, and no mistake. Better than any physic, she is,' declared an elderly fisherman, whose boat had rammed the harbour wall in a storm, and deposited him on the deck with such force that it broke his leg. 'No offence meant, Doctor,' he grinned in apology to the houseman, whose white-coated figure passing by the end of the bed reminded him that his enthusiasm for Berry's broadcasting might be interpreted as a slight on the medical services.

'None taken,' the houseman twinkled. 'We should all

miss her, if she left.'

He wished, with a regret as genuine as that of his patient, that the charm he used to such good effect on the junior nurses might have an equal impact on the seemingly unimpressed Miss Baker.

The name Berry suited her, he reflected. It went with her small, snub nose, liberally dusted with freckles, which she had tried in vain since the age of fourteen to disguise or otherwise get rid of. It went with her short brown bob, lit by glints of gold like an autumn hedgerow, and which she brushed straight back behind her ears to frame her sensitive, heart-shaped face, with the clear hazel eyes that were such a candid mirror of her feelings, and tended to turn smoky under stress.

He was glad to see that they turned smoky far less often nowadays.

Her name went with her smile. The houseman's own lips curved as he thought of her smile, and the small, even teeth it revealed, like a bright glint of sunshine in her mobile face.

The smile flashed now as Berry spoke into the microphone, as if her listeners in the wards below could see it and be cheered by its friendly warmth.

'Goodnight. Sleep tight,' she called. 'And if you can't sleep, think about tomorrow. Remember, it's the last card in our current bingo game. Who is going to win it this week?'

She left the question to occupy the minds of the ones who failed to woo sleep, and switched off the microphone. Pushing it to the back of the table, she swung round to face her companions in the small broadcasting studio attached to the hospital.

'I'm off now,' John Barclay announced. ''Night, Berry. See you tomorrow.'

He was already on his feet as he spoke, and reaching for his jacket from the hook behind the door. 'We're giving Mr Prentiss a lift home,' he added, the 'we' including his wife, who would be going off duty now at the change of shifts on casualty.

The smile still lingered on Berry's lips as she echoed, 'See you tomorrow, John. Goodnight, Mr Prentiss. And thanks.'

She rose and stretched her cramped limbs as the two men went out together. The mayor was popular with everyone in the lively coastal town of Aldermouth, and as usual he had managed a discussion that would be of interest to all their listener patients, who were drawn from an area that derived its living from land, sea, and the holiday industry.

There would be plenty of reaction to the broadcast when she visited the wards tomorrow, Berry guessed, as she buttoned on her woolly, and bent to pick up her handbag from the floor beside her chair.

She locked the door and dropped the key into the porter's office before she went to make sure that Trish was in the glass-walled cubicle which made a neat divider between men's surgical on the one side and women's surgical on the other.

'Come into the goldfish bowl,' the ward sister maligned her spotless quarters. 'All the patients are tucked up for the night, so I can take a breather for a while.'

'Why do you always grumble about your office? I think it's a super little place. You can see every inch of the ward on either side of you, without having to move a step away from your desk.'

'That's just the trouble. I feel as if I'm on show in a glass case. I've got a dozen patients on each side of me, with nothing to do all day except lie in bed and wait to get better. Watching me is their main occupation. If I held hands with one of the consultants, it would be all over the hospital in seconds.'

'So would the black eye your husband would give to any consultant who tried,' Berry grinned.

Trish was married to an engineer who, in his spare moments, was a useful rugby scrum-half, and they were still happily married after ten years, with no sign of the longed-for child.

'Did you manage to find the seat your hassock belonged to?' Trish asked, spooning coffee granules into two mugs.

'Yes, thanks. I was glad of your cloak, too. You were right, it was cold going across the car park.'

Her shoulder still felt curiously hot where the stranger had held it, and impulsively she added,

'There was a man in the chapel. He spoke as if he belonged to St Luke's, but he's new to me.'

'Oh, yes? You intrigue me mightily. Describe him.'

Berry got no further than, 'Very tall. Slim. Dark auburn hair, and vivid green eyes,' when Trish exclaimed,

'Julian Vyse!'

'Who? I don't remember hearing his name mentioned. And I've certainly not met him before, around the hospital.'

'You wouldn't. He's new here. He came while you were away on holiday, and you haven't been likely to meet him since you've been back, because he operates in the mornings, and you don't get here until the afternoon.'

'Then why . . .?'

'Today he's had to change his lists over, and operate

in the afternoon, because one of the theatres is out of action. He's had a particularly full list today, too. Several of his patients are in my wards now.' She nodded to the dimly lit lines of beds on either side of her office.

'I hope for your sake he isn't as grim to work for as he looks,' Berry sympathised. 'Or haven't you had time to find out yet?'

'I don't need to, as a matter of fact. I worked with Julian when he was at the General at Peterhead. I got to know him pretty well when he was a lot lower down the scale than he is now, so his abrasive manner doesn't bother me. He's a perfectionist, and they're never easy to work for. He doesn't suffer fools gladly, and anyone who makes the same mistake twice gets the sharp edge of his tongue, but he's a brilliant surgeon. He's good with the juniors, too. He's amazingly patient about explaining to them what he's doing, and why. All the junior nursing staff at the General were dazzled by him, and adored him from afar.' Her eyes twinkled. 'He doesn't seem to have lost his touch. Two of my juniors are already going around with that dazed look on their faces.'

'Silly idiots,' Berry snorted, and felt thankful that she herself was nowadays immune from such senseless behaviour.

'Oh, I don't know. The feminine heart's a susceptible organ. I've seen Julian Vyse in the theatre, stripped for action down to his waist before putting on his gown. Wow! That man has the torso of a Tarzan. It's enough to make any young and inexperienced nurse keel over at first sight.'

'They ought to have more sense.'

'Don't be so critical. It might happen to you, one day. Just wait until Mr Right appears on the horizon.'

'I'll let you know when it happens.'

'You won't need to. The hospital grapevine will know about it before you do,' Trish laughed. 'It's a lot more reliable than your broadcasting system. It doesn't miss out any of the juicy titbits.'

Berry grimaced. She was well aware of the grapevine's power. She had been the subject of gossiping tongues herself, once, but Trish was not to know that, so she parried lightly, 'When the time comes, I'll make sure that the grapevine spreads only accurate information. But don't start looking out fancy wedding-hats, because it'll be for ever before you'll need to wear one, so far as I'm concerned.'

In spite of herself, a bitter note crept into Berry's voice, and Trish gave her a considering look as she answered, 'I don't believe that. You'll end up happily married, some day.'

'I've been married.'

Berry braked hard on her tongue, but she was not in time to prevent the words from coming out, and her indrawn breath made an audible skid-mark in the surprised silence.

'You're a dark horse, I must say. I've never heard you speak of a Mr Baker.'

'His name wasn't Baker. I reverted to using my maiden name afterwards.'

Berry felt like kicking herself. Since coming to live in Aldermouth she had discussed her past life with no one, not even Trish. It had taken her a long time to come to terms with it herself, and now she had at last got to the stage of regaining most of her lost confidence she did not want her still-fragile self-esteem to be shattered again by hospital gossip.

Trish said quietly, 'Didn't it work?'

'No.'

Berry's closed expression discouraged further questioning and, after a long look at the withdrawn face of her visitor, Trish sidetracked, 'Have another mug of coffee. If I wasn't on duty, and you weren't driving, I might offer you something a bit stronger. But, since I am, and you are, it'll have to be two spoonfuls of instant, instead of one, to make up. I could do with my own coffee double strength tonight, after the day I've had.'

'Why, what's happened?' Berry felt grateful to Trish for her tactful change of subject.

'Julian had three young children on his list today, and I've had to put them among the adults on my ward. It's no place for a very young child, and he was pretty caustic about St Luke's having no children's ward, but there was no help for it.'

'He's got a cheek! He can't have been here for many weeks. It's like his nerve to start throwing his weight about already. St Luke's has managed without a children's ward until now.

'Managed, just about describes it. Julian's right. It isn't good to have to put young children in with adults.'

Berry frowned. 'I've never understood the lack, myself. St Luke's seems to have plenty of room. Look at the space we've been allocated for our studio. We could actually manage with far less. Not that I'm not grateful for such comfortable quarters,' she hastened to add.

'If St Luke's was paying for the broadcasting service, instead of it being funded by voluntary contributions, you wouldn't have anything at all,' Trish retorted. 'We've got stacks of room, but no money. There's a small wing here that's been closed for ages, and it would be ideal for a children's ward. It's self-contained, with one big square room sufficient to hold at least a dozen cots, and a smaller one next to it that would make a lovely playroom. It wouldn't take all that much to set it up, but . . .' She shrugged. 'What's the use of wishing?'

She collected up the now empty mugs, as the sonorous chimes of the parish clock echoed across the darkened town. Berry counted them out loud. 'Ten, eleven, twelve . . . I didn't realise it was so late. Wish now, Trish,' she exclaimed impulsively. 'It's midnight. Isn't that when all wishes are supposed to come true?'

'If only I could believe that.'

'Go on, then, put it to the test. I thought all Irish people believed in magic.'

Not being a Celt herself, Berry felt no obligation to adhere to such beliefs, and any magic for her had long since been destroyed, she reflected, as she shivered her way later across the now deserted tarmac to where her car stood in its accustomed slot.

As she walked, she felt a burning resentment against the man in the hospital chapel, that he should, however indirectly, stir up memories of her past, just when she was beginning to believe that she had put them behind her.

She garaged her car, and let herself into her flat, feeling the evergreen sense of pleasure as she walked through the rooms which she herself had chosen and furnished.

Tonight, however, she felt restless, and her much-prized refuge did not give her the peace it usually offered. At this late, or early, hour, she was undecided which, the empty rooms seem to be peopled by ghosts that she had come to believe were safely laid.

It was Trish, too, with all her blarney about happy marriages. Berry's lips took on a cynical twist. If her own experience was anything to go by, happiness was an illusion that did not last.

Her eyes sought the clock on the wall, and some of her customary humour reasserted itself. It was long gone midnight now, so it was too late for wishful thinking. Several years too late, in her own case. The only good thing that had come out of it for her was that, having learned from experience, she would not make the same mistake again.

In spite of the hour, Trish's strong coffee had induced a spurious alertness that would not allow her to rest, and she undressed slowly, and lay in the darkness in company with the ghosts, who should no longer have the power to torment her, as something had obviously done to Julian Vyse that evening.

Berry wondered idly what it could be. A vision of the consultant's agonised face rose to meet her. It must be something of disastrous proportions to make him look like that. His whole bearing exuded strength and confidence. Trish had said he did not suffer fools gladly, and neither, Berry suspected, would he suffer anything so to disturb his peace of mind, unless it was of major consequence to him personally.

So, what had disturbed him tonight? What major disaster had so rocked him, had made him look as he had for those brief moments in the chapel before he caught sight of her and pulled the shutters down?

Effectively shutting in whatever it was, and just as effectively shutting Berry out.

Her own personal disaster had been catastrophic. It had shattered her life, and in some areas Berry was still picking up the pieces, and she could not view kindly anyone who reminded her of that part of her life which she only wanted to forget.

For the first few months of her marriage to Chris, Berry had been blissfully happy. She was a very young eighteen, and hopelessly in love.

Chris had a silver tongue, and he knew how to use it to good effect, and Berry was an easy target.

She had little knowledge of the world, and even less of men. She was orphaned at an early age, and her crusty, bachelor guardian had abdicated his responsibility to various boarding-schools in whose care he left her, even during the school holidays.

When the time came for her to leave the closed and essentially feminine community she was accustomed to, Berry was the perfect innocent abroad.

Chris was twenty-seven, and light-years ahead of her in experience. His work as a salesman often took him away for several nights at a time, and during those periods their small flat became a barren desert to Berry, but the coming-home times made it all worth while.

He would sweep her into his arms and kiss her until her face was rosy, and they would eat the special supper Berry had taken such pains to prepare, which Chris always declared was nectar and ambrosia because she had cooked it for him.

Sometimes, when he had a run of good orders, he would take her out on the town, and they would dance, and Chris would promise her the earth, dangling their future like a shining carrot in front of her dazzled eyes.

Afterwards, they would go back home to the flat, and Berry would lie in Chris's arms, and dream.

But every dreamer has to awaken at some time, and Berry's awakening was as rude as it was final. It came one morning with a knock on the front door. She opened it to find a woman, not much older than herself, standing on the mat, and with a very young baby in her arms.

'I'm Chris's wife,' she announced.

After that, the dreams turned into nightmares for Berry. Not long afterwards, yet another 'wife' turned up from a different part of the country, and Chris's carefree days as a salesman came to an abrupt end.

The only good thing to come out of the whole dreadful affair, from Berry's point of view, was that Chris had not given her a child, as he had the other two women, and she was able to cut completely free from him, with no reminders except her shattered confidence.

Her solicitor told her when it was all over, 'You mustn't feel in any way to blame. You were not to know. The guilt lies entirely with your husband ... er, I mean ...'

Bitterly, Berry knew exactly what he meant. And no matter what he said, she *did* feel guilty, and bitterly ashamed. What had happened with Chris had trampled on all her principles and, although it was through no fault of her own that it happened, Berry felt despoiled, and suffered a lack of confidence in herself that was a cross she would have to bear for a long time to come.

She tried to explain all this to the solicitor, but he thrust her stammered words aside with a bluff, 'Put it all behind you, my dear. Make a new life for yourself. Forget it.'

Sound advice, Berry knew, but it was not so easy to put into practice. It might have been over for the solicitor—just another case to be filed away and forgotten. But for Berry it was only the beginning, and however much she wanted to forget it, she discovered to her cost that she was not allowed to.

The sudden silences when she came across a group of people talking together told her they were talking about her. The snide remarks. 'Good morning Mrs ... oh, I forgot, it's Miss, isn't it?' The sniggers, not quite hidden behind raised hands.

The gossip was almost as cruel to Berry's sensitive nature as Chris had been. And he had been cruel, she acknowledged with belated honesty.

When he had teased her with spiders, knowing how she dreaded them. She had always forgiven him afterwards when he'd dried her tears with kisses, and promised to remember in future. But he never had.

The gossips seemed to derive the same sadistic enjoyment from their own form of cruelty, and the court case gave them plenty to feed on, because Chris had resorted to embezzlement in order to fund his personal harem, which dragged out the case and made it worse, and his subsequent punishment more severe.

It might not have cut quite so deeply if Berry had had a family to lean on, but her guardian was all she had, and she knew better than to turn to him for sympathy. She wished she could crawl into a hole and hide.

Instead, she gritted her teeth and braved the gossips, and as soon as the case was over she gave up the tenancy of the flat and moved right away, where she could bind her wounds in decent privacy, and hope they would leave no permanent scars.

She had no idea where she wanted to go, so she solved the dilemma by sticking a pin in a map, as far away from her present location as her closed eyes and fumbling fingers could guess at.

The pinpoint found Aldermouth, and within a month she was installed in her present flat and had found the perfect antidote to her own troubles in her present job with the hospital radio service.

It took her out and about, meeting people, which suited her friendly nature. But now she kept a firm curb on that nature, which puzzled many who would have liked to make that friendship closer.

She reverted to her maiden name, and was, to all intents, a single woman again, and single was how she intended to remain in future.

Her incursion into matrimony was a one-off, she vowed, and from now on her flat, and her present busy lifestyle, was all she wanted. Tonight, however, for the first time, the flat seemed unaccountably lonely.

The clock in the living-room chimed two, and Berry groaned as she plumped up her pillows for the umpteenth time. To try to send the ghosts packing she forced her mind to concentrate on her conversation with Trish earlier that evening. What had the ward sister said?

We've got stacks of room, but no money. And, it wouldn't take all that much to set it up.

Stacks of room, but no money.

The phrase wandered round and round in Berry's head with irritating persistence, like a mosquito that refused to be swatted. And when at last she slipped into sleep, Julian Vyse's stern face followed her, taking the place of the mosquito.

His penetrating green eyes bored into her own, and his commanding voice echoed through her dreams, telling her in no uncertain terms to, 'Raise the money. Raise the money.'

# CHAPTER TWO

BERRY woke the next morning with a plan vaguely forming in her mind.

She refused to acknowledge that it had been put there by the man in the chapel last night, although his image had persisted in disturbing her rest until, in exasperation, she had an earlier-than-usual shower and cup of coffee to rid her mind of the wraiths of the previous day.

Her conversation with Trish was still occupying her mind when she reached the hospital that afternoon and sought out her friend in the canteen, where she guessed that Trish would be having her usual pre-duty cup of tea.

'I've been thinking around what we were talking about last night,' she began without preliminary.

'Men,' Trish grinned.

'No, you ass.' Berry shied away from the memory of her gaffe last night. 'I mean, the children's ward.'

'What children's ward?' Trish retorted darkly. 'Do you *have* to rub it in? One of the toddlers Julian operated on yesterday had a bad night. Poor little scrap wants his mum, and he kept the whole ward awake all night, yelling for her.'

'Why didn't you call her in?'

'Because she's got four others to look after, and no husband at home to help. Her man's a deep-sea fisherman, and he's away from home a lot of the time. We get a good many children like that, and it turns their mothers into virtually one-parent families for weeks on end.'

'All the more reason why you should have a special children's ward, where they can't disturb the other patients if they happen to be restless.'

'I'm too old to believe in fairy-tales any more. Where do you suppose the money will come from?'

'We could raise it between us.'

Momentarily, an image of a lean, tormented face flashed across Berry's mind, and a deep voice repeated, 'Raise the money. Raise the money.'

Julian Vyse had had a more telling effect upon her than she realised, Berry thought. She was borrowing his words, even though they were only dreams, and not real.

'Like you'll clear the national debt, I suppose?' Trish scoffed.

Her disbelief was the reverse of encouraging, and it goaded Berry in the opposite direction. She insisted stubbornly, 'We *could* do it, Trish, if we spread the word about. And how better to do that than through the hospital radio system?' Now the die was cast, she warmed to the idea. 'The patients and their relatives would rally round, and the word would soon spread. We could get in touch with the mayor. I know he'd help, he's an absolute poppet. We had him on our programme yesterday.'

'It'll cost a bomb.'

'It needn't. You said yourself it wouldn't take all that much to set it up.'

'I meant all that much, compared with the oil revenue.' Trish's rejoinder was dry. 'It would cost thousands. It wouldn't only be the cost of the cots and the medical equipment. There would be all the decorating. Those rooms are badly neglected. They've been closed for years.'

'My neighbour's in that line of business. I might be able to get the materials at cost price.'

'Labour's expensive.'

'We'll rope in volunteers, then the labour needn't cost us anything at all. I wield a pretty good paint brush, even though I say it myself.'

'It's a huge undertaking.'

'Oh, come on, Trish, don't be such a pessimist! Remember David and Goliath.'

Why did the names of those two ancient combatants bring to mind Julian Vyse's lean six feet plus, dwarfing her own slight figure in the chapel last night? Berry thrust the image aside impatiently, and reminded the ward sister, 'You wished at midnight, didn't you? Can't you see, this could be your wish coming true?'

Now that she had put her idea into bald words, Berry herself felt a qualm about taking on such a huge undertaking, but she stoutly refused to allow her doubts to show in front of Trish.

'You've almost convinced me,' the ward sister admitted, and there was a dawning hope in her face as she glanced down at her watch and exclaimed, 'I must fly, or I'll be late taking over from my opposite number.'

'So must I.' Berry thrust back her chair. 'It's the big night tonight. I've got to announce the name of the bingo winner for this week.'

'It isn't me, I suppose?'

'No, it's the elderly seaman with the broken leg. Come to think of it, I can ask him for a donation. He might like to start our Children's Ward Fund off with some of his winnings. There, I've even got a title for our campaign already. How's that for speed?'

Berry used some speed herself to accelerate up the stairs, and she laid her scheme before her radio producer. John was also chairman of the hospital board, and to her delight he greeted her idea with unqualified approval.

'It's great thinking, Berry. I'm due at a committee meeting in five minutes. I'll put it to them for approval, but I'm sure I'll have no trouble in getting their clearance for you to go ahead.'

The approval must have been unanimous, because it was not long before John rang back to the studio with the news she had been waiting for.

'Go ahead, Berry. The committee's backing you all the way.'

Jubilantly, Berry made her way down to the wards to take the elderly seaman his five pounds bingo prize.

'You're doing a great job, love,' he praised her when she told him about the new campaign. 'Start off your fund with this.' His gnarled fingers pressed his prize money firmly back into Berry's palm. 'As soon as I'm back on my feet again, I'll send you some more,' he promised.

Back in the studio to start her stint of broadcasting, Berry carefully put the prized donation into a neatly labelled box.

'You're ambitious,' John teased her when he returned from the meeting and saw its size. 'You need a slit in the top, though, so that people can put in their money themselves.'

He cut her a slit with the office scissors, and pushed a note through it himself with the gruff excuse, 'I've got to make sure it's big enough, haven't I?'

The box itself proved to be not nearly big enough in the end, and John had to bring the scissors into play again, and cut another slit in an even larger box lid.

Berry announced the winner of the bingo prize, and to the glee of the elderly fisherman she also announced how he had spent the money. It made the perfect run-up to her appeal.

'Rally round, folks,' she urged her listeners. 'St Luke's needs a children's ward, and needs one badly, and soon. They're your children. For their sake, it's up to us all to pull together, and give them what they need.'

She put her heart and soul into her plea, and it came through in her voice, but even Berry did not envisage such an instant response to her broadcast. Within an hour of her appeal, her first collecting box was full, and the second was rapidly filling.

A new spirit galvanised the patients. They forgot their aches and pains and rose to the challenge. Those who were able to walk tottered round the wards collecting from those who could not.

One enterprising lad with a sense of humour begged a bed-pan liner from an amused staff nurse, and presented it later to Berry, filled to overflowing with money he had extracted from relatives and friends at visiting time.

'Count the money, and I'll lock it in the safe for you tonight,' offered the delighted matron. 'As soon as the bank opens in the morning, I'll have a special account made out for the fund, and you can broadcast the number in case people want to send in money anonymously.'

'It's taken off in a big way, Berry,' John enthused.

'Big is right.' Berry looked awestruck. 'We've got

three hundred and fifty-eight pounds and six pence already, and I only announced the appeal just over an hour ago.'

By the end of the evening the total had more than doubled, and Berry admitted to feeling slightly scared at the speed with which her good idea had taken off.

'I didn't realise what I was letting myself in for,' she confessed to Trish over their habitual late-night cup of coffee together.

'You can't stop now. You mustn't. We need that ward, Berry.'

'I don't intend to stop. You'll get your ward, don't worry.'

But it was Berry herself who did the worrying as she went home afterwards and prepared for bed in a sober mood. Her new-found confidence, that nowadays took in its stride her work in the broadcasting studio, began to waver at the enormity of this other, much larger project.

She was confident in her own niche behind the microphone, but had she built up enough confidence yet in herself as a person to be able to cope with this new, and hitherto unexplored world of organising something on such a grand scale?

Her impulsive suggestion seemed to have blown up in her face, and suddenly she did not feel sure if she was capable of handling the resulting explosion.

Her cruel experience with Chris, and the humiliating aftermath, had left deep scars which still pained her, enough to make her cry out loud in her sleep, 'I don't know if I can,' when a deep voice pursued her, demanding, 'Raise the money.'

When Berry arrived at the hospital the next after-noon, Trish greeted her with, 'There's no time for us to have a cup of tea together today. Julian wants to see you as soon as you arrive.' She added as an afterthought, 'Matron said to let you know she's sent a note up to the studio for you, as well.'

'That will be the number of the bank account she promised to take out for the ward fund,' Berry guessed. 'What does Julian Vyse want to see me for? Anyway, what's the matter with him coming to see me in the studio?' she rebelled. 'I'm not one of his nursing staff, to come running whenever he deigns to lift a finger!'

She still smarted at the easy way she had obeyed him in the chapel, and she did not intend that it should become a habit. Easy compliance was something that belonged to the Berry of the past.

'He hasn't got time to come to the studio, Berry. He's due in theatre again in half an hour. One of the other surgeons has gone down with a tummy bug, and Julian's having to take over his workload at short notice. Go and see him, there's a lamb.'

Trish broke off and turned to help a young mother with a baby in her arms and a toddler clutching at her skirts, who wailed with rising desperation, 'Mummy, I want to . . .'

'Third floor, second room along,' Trish called over her shoulder to Berry as she bore her charges in the required direction, and Berry turned reluctantly towards the lift, with her question still unanswered.

What did Julian Vyse want to see her for?

She was tempted to ignore his high-handed summons. The consultants' rooms overlooked the car park, she knew, and it was more than likely that Julian Vyse had seen her arrive. It would serve as a salutary lesson to his arrogance if she failed to appear.

On the other hand, Berry's own lively bump of curiosity demanded that she find out what he wanted of her. It might be some snippet of information that she could use in her broadcasts and, if so, she could not afford to miss it.

Almost without direction, her finger pressed the lift button for the third floor, and within seconds the cage trundled to a halt in front of her, and the gates opened.

The reversal of her usual fortunes with the elusive inter-floor transport was almost like an omen, she thought. It was as if Julian Vyse had willed the lift to come and fetch her, in order to make sure that she obeyed his summons, and Berry could not suppress a sudden sense of being trapped as the gates clanged shut on her, and the lift bore her upwards, towards his room.

She checked the doors in the corridor. Second room along, Trish had said. She raised her hand, and gave the wooden oblong a businesslike knock.

'Come,' a voice responded, and Berry thought ruefully, He doesn't sound any more approachable now than he was the other night.

She came, and her eyes winged to meet the alert green gaze fixed on her from the other side of a wide expanse of dark oak desk, which was set in the opposite corner of the room.

Julian Vyse rose from his seat as Berry paused just inside the door, and he said, with a touch of asperity, as if he might be talking to a junior nurse, 'Come right inside, and close the door behind you. I can't talk to you from the other end of the room.'

Putting her in the wrong, Berry realised wrathfully, before she even had the chance to wish him good afternoon, which she no longer felt inclined to do. Her lips set in a tight line. If he could dispense with the normal courtesies, so could she.

'Sister Connelly asked me to come and see you,' she clipped, emphasising that she was here to oblige Trish, and not to obey him. At the same time, Berry glanced at her watch, silently telling him that she had not got all day to spare either, and the green eyes flickered, noting, and dismissing, her hint.

'Sit down.' He moved a chair forward.

Unwillingly, Berry sat, trying to look more relaxed than she felt. The alert green eyes had a most curious effect upon her. Now that she could view him in broad daylight, Berry saw the reason why the St Luke's new senior consultant had had such an impact upon Trish's junior nursing staff.

He was devastatingly attractive. And knew it, Berry decided caustically.

He held his head high in a proud carriage that made him look even taller than he had appeared in the chapel and, in spite of the armour with which Berry had surrounded herself since Chris, she felt her spine tingle as she looked at him.

Vibes flowed from him that discovered all the chinks and, no matter how she gloried in her present single blessedness, she was still a woman, and an essentially feminine one, and Julian Vyse exuded a vital masculine attraction that drew an instinctive response from Berry's curling nerve-ends.

It was a purely physical attraction, but no less unwelcome for that, and angrily Berry slapped it into submission. If Julian Vyse imagined that his good looks carried any weight with her he was very much mistaken!

Instead of retreating behind the big desk, as she

expected him to do, the consultant captured another chair for himself, and came to sit in front of Berry.

Right in front. Their knees almost touched, and instinctively she smoothed her cheerful red corduroy skirt further over her silk-stockinged legs. This evening she had come prepared for a change in temperature, with a white polo-necked sweater and a thick woolly jacket of the same red as her skirt, and the bright outfit made her look like a small robin perched on the deep green plush of the chair.

It also made her look several years younger than her modest twenty-three, and her host's lips curved slightly. Berry stared at him, startled, and thought, What a difference it makes, when he smiles.

It was only half a smile. An apology for the real thing. Just the same, it made his face look younger, and marginally less forbidding, but still far from approachable. Berry felt glad that she was not one of his patients, but perhaps he behaved differently towards them.

Refusing to return the smile, she pinned a politely enquiring look on her face, and steeled herself to wait. Julian Vyse had asked—nay, ordered—her to come to see him, so it was up to him to state the reason why. She refused to be reduced to asking, and so give him the advantage.

He had that already, she conceded reluctantly, since she had come at his bidding, and the admission that she had lowered her flag even this far, to oblige Trish, was an added irritant.

He broke the silence abruptly. 'Sister Connelly tells me you're about to present St Luke's with a children's ward.'

He made it sound like now, this very minute. As if she

were Lady Bountiful, distributing instant largesse. The thinly veiled sarcasm in his voice brought a bright spot of colour to Berry's either cheek, and she kept her temper with an effort.

She was not on this lordly creature's staff, so she had no need to endure his sharp tongue. Deftly she caught his bullets, and threw them back with energy.

'She mentioned the need. She said you weren't happy about putting young children in an adult ward.'

Berry stopped abruptly and bit her lip. She had not meant to put it quite like that. It sounded as if the idea had come from him in the first place, and it had not. It had come from her, and she was determined that he should acknowledge the fact.

Julian Vyse took up her words alertly.

'St Luke's must have needed the ward long before I arrived on the scene.'

Berry bridled. St Luke's had operated with superb efficiency before he had arrived, and it was sheer conceit on his part to assume otherwise. She said stiffly, 'St Luke's has always been aware of the need, but there hasn't been the money to pay for it.'

'And now I've kicked up a fuss about it, you've decided to stir yourselves, and do something about it?'

He grabbed the ball firmly back into his own court, and Berry gritted her teeth. Round one to him. Before she could think up a satisfactory answer, he went on, 'Have you got any idea how much money you'll need to raise, to pay for the ward?'

Various sums had occurred to Berry during the course of a long and sleepless night, each one more frightening than the last, but she had to admit, 'Not yet. There hasn't been time. I only had the idea yesterday.'

'There's no time to drag feet. The need for this ward is urgent.'

'I know that.' The cheek of the man, to accuse her of dragging her feet, when it had been her own idea in the first place!

Berry drew in a deep, steadying breath, and said, 'I'm coming in to the hospital tomorrow morning, to look at the rooms, and measure them up.'

She had not intended to do it quite so soon but, faced with the challenge of those piercing green eyes, she made up her mind quickly. Tomorrow was Saturday, and she had a free morning, with nothing much else to do, so she might as well fill it with that.

'Why not measure up tonight?'

He was goading her, and Berry flashed, 'I want to do the job properly, and late at night is no time to start measuring up rooms.'

'I'm working late tonight.'

'I'm not,' she rebelled. 'I need to see the rooms in daylight, to assess them for colours and so on, and to find out from the maintenance staff if any structural alterations need to be done before decorating starts.'

'I've got a paint colour chart here. Let's have a look at it now. It'll save you time tomorrow.'

He reached out a long arm behind him, captured a concertinaed card from the desk and, to Berry's consternation, instead of using the desktop on which to spread it out, he hitched his chair forward the short couple of inches necessary to bring his knees into contact with her own, and made a long lap on which to smooth out the chart between them.

The touch of his knees was as electric as his hand on her shoulder had been, and it was all Berry could do not to skid her chair backwards, away from it. She would not have been surprised if twin scorch marks had taken the pile from the red corduroy of her skirt.

It took all her strength of mind to resist the panic that invaded her at his touch. Her eyes flew upwards to his face, and met his quizzical green stare, a stare that saw what she was feeling, knew what she was thinking, and challenged her to stay where she was.

Hurriedly, Berry dropped her eyes to the chart. The colours seemed to dance in front of her eyes.

She would have given a week's salary to stop the colour that flooded her throat and cheeks, rising in a rosy tide until she felt convinced there must be little difference in shade between her skirt and her skin, and hated Julian Vyse for what she knew had been a deliberate and calculated move, made on purpose to confuse her and put her at a disadvantage.

Her skin prickled as his hand smoothed the chart flat across her lap and his own, his fingers lingering over the colours on her side. Long, sensitive surgeon's fingers, with neatly rounded filbert nails that touched each bright oblong on the chart, unhurriedly as if he was giving consideration to the colours.

Not because they might be suitable for the ward, Berry felt angrily certain, but only to heighten her discomfort to the pitch when she would be able to tolerate it no longer, and would agree to whatever he might suggest for the ward, simply in order to get away from him.

During the long, restless hours of last night, Berry had wondered just what she was taking on by launching the ward project. Now, she discovered that she was taking on Julian Vyse as well, and the second prospect seemed to be even more daunting than the first.

He pressurised her with a speed that was little short of merciless. The colour chart was but one example of the way he was already getting himself involved.

He demanded the playroom within a month for children who came in as day patients, and the ward itself within an impossibly short time afterwards.

'I can't work miracles!' Berry gasped.

'How do you know, until you try? I've told you, it's no use dragging feet.'

A furious anger stirred in Berry. The children's ward was her idea. And this man, this self-opinionated, domineering creature, making her pulses behave in the most unseemly manner, was taking it over and telling her what she must do about it. Treating her, in fact, as if she was a mere cipher, there to obey his every dictate.

It was the same with the campaign committee.

'The mayor's got all the machinery,' he pointed out. 'He's the best person to cope with the publicity, and has more contacts with the local business houses than any one of us. He'll make an ideal secretary, and Matron will take over the purse-strings I'm sure, so you've got your treasurer.'

'I suppose you see yourself as chairman?' Berry made no attempt to hide the bite in her voice, but to her surprise he shook his head.

'No. I'm too busy to serve on a committee.'

'We're all busy. It's just as difficult for me to leave my work for this as it is for you.' He spoke as if he were the only one who ever did any work, Berry fulminated.

'Your work is life-enhancing. Mine is life-saving. And, in any case, I'm booked to go on a lecture tour in America at the end of the month. It'll take me out of the country for several weeks, so I shouldn't be able to fill the role of chairman satisfactorily.'

'No doubt you've decided who's going to fill it instead.'

He seemed to have the whole campaign already mapped out and ready to spring into action, but he ignored her sarcasm and nodded.

'Actually, I'd thought of a chair*person*. A lady,' he said gravely. 'You, in fact. I think you'd make a charming chairperson.'

And, rising to his feet, he drew Berry up to stand in front of him, and imprinted the seal of his approval full on her lips with his own.

Shock sent Berry rigid. She felt too surprised to resist. The last person to kiss her like this had been Chris. But not like this. Not even remotely like this. Julian Vyse's kiss had a quality like nothing she had experienced with Chris. It lanced through her like a lightning bolt, aimed with deliberation for the most telling effect, and for a few seconds Berry stood transfixed.

Piercing green eyes, and dark auburn waves, filled her vision, and his lips bored down on to hers with a pressure that set them on fire. The pain exploded Berry into action.

'Let me go!' With furious arms, she fought herself free and backed away from him, wiping insulting hands across her burning mouth.

'Why the outrage?' His eyes mocked her fury. 'Most girls like being kissed.'

'I'm not most girls,' Berry spat. 'Keep your kisses for the student nurses. They might like them. I don't.'

'Do you think it's below your dignity as a chairperson to be kissed?'

'I just don't like it, and that's that. And I haven't agreed to be chairperson, yet. The mayor and Matron may not want to be on the committee, either.'

'Ring and ask them. And while you're about it, invite all the committee members to my house to dinner tomorrow evening. Seven-thirty will be fine. Matron knows the address. We can beat out a plan of campaign between us then.'

'You mean you'll have a plan already mapped out, and expect the rest of us to just rubber-stamp it without argument!'

'It's time someone injected a sense of urgency into your sleepy little town,' he taunted, and dropped a light kiss on the tip of Berry's small, freckled nose.

It injected his sense of urgency into her feet, and it was all she could do to prevent herself from breaking into a run as she hurried along the corridor, edgily aware of his eyes following her retreat from his room.

Berry turned on to the stairs rather than wait for the lift and endure the knife-prick of his stare a moment longer, but caution demanded that she slow down and get her breath back before she reached the studio. John was not deceived, however, when she reached her desk and began to fumble among the papers waiting for her on its top.

'What's up?' her producer wanted to know, and, conscious that she could not hide her ruffled feelings, Berry let fly.

'It's that man. That new consultant. He wants the children's ward yesterday! He seems to think I can wave some sort of magic wand, and produce it, just like that.'

She carefully omitted to mention by what means the consultant had tried to achieve his object, and hoped

John's friendly eyes were not so far-seeing as the green ones she had just left.

'You must admit, Julian Vyse is a go-getter. St Luke's really needs someone like him, to stir things up. The other consultants were all getting on in years. Now they've retired, and we've got a younger team at the top, they'll have more energy to make improvements.'

In Berry's eyes, Julian Vyse was *not* one of the improvements! She needed him like she needed a hole in the head, but she bit back her comments, turned away, and opened the top envelope on the pile of papers. It was Matron's note, containing the expected bank account number.

'I'll broadcast this right away.' Berry turned to her microphone, but John checked her as she was about to switch it on.

'Hang on a minute. We've had some more donations come in during the day. Here's the latest update on the total.' He handed her a slip of paper, and the figures written on the bottom made Berry's eyes widen. 'We'll make a daily announcement of the latest figure,' John suggested. 'It'll keep the interest going. Now we've got the pot on the boil, it'll pay us to keep the heat turned up.'

Julian Vyse had told her much the same thing, but it sounded better in Berry's ears coming from John. Silently she held out her hand for the slip of paper, and for the next couple of hours she was able to put all thoughts of the consultant to the back of her mind.

She was kept busy with announcements, reading a story for the children, sending out local titbits of news, and playing the usual crop of dedications for the adults, and then obligingly John took over from her while she made her telephone calls.

In spite of her uncharitable wish that they would decline, both the matron and the mayor agreed to take on their new roles, and in spite of the short notice were able to accept the consultant's dinner invitation for the following evening.

'That only leaves you to find a chairman for the committee,' John observed when she'd finished. 'Perhaps Julian will take on the job?'

'He can't. He's got a lecture tour in the States at the end of the month. It'll keep him out of the country for several weeks.'

Berry found herself yearning for those weeks to come. With Julian Vyse out of her way she would be free to put her brain-child into action without having the consultant breathing down her neck and trying to dictate every action she took.

The knowledge that so far he had succeeded rankled badly.

'Did he suggest anyone else who might be suitable?'

Even John tacitly concurred that Julian Vyse should be the one to do the suggesting, and not herself, and Berry said stiffly, 'He suggested me.'

'You?' John took one look at the fire in Berry's eyes, and added hastily, 'I don't see why not.'

Clearly he did, and Berry's frustration boiled over. Right at that moment, she felt she loathed all men.

'I'm not a helpless female, John.'

'I know,' John soothed. 'But this idea of yours ...'

'So you do acknowledge that it was my idea?'

'Of course I do. Don't be so tetchy. But it's a very different thing, having an inspiration, from putting it into practice. You must admit that this campaign's gaining momentum with the speed of an avalanche. We haven't even started any publicity yet, and it's all over the town already. Some of the donations we've had in today have come from the business population.'

Berry's grimace was rueful. 'You don't need to tell me.'

'Then you must see that, once the mayor's publicity machine really gets going, the whole thing is going to turn into something a lot bigger than you envisaged. It'll need someone very strong-minded indeed to be able to control it.'

'A man, in fact,' Berry answered bitterly.

'Or a real battleaxe from the fair sex. And you, Rowanberry, are far too sweet to be a battleaxe.'

'You are an ass, John.' Berry's ready sense of humour reasserted itself, and she giggled.

'I know. But seriously, Berry, with a project of this size, the committee could well do with having two chairmen, instead of just the one.'

'Then come in with me, as joint chairman, and we'll turn it into the hospital radio appeal, and make the studio its headquarters.'

And, at a stroke, remove control of the appeal from the domineering hands of Julian Vyse and put it back where it belonged, into her own, Berry added with silent satisfaction.

For a second or two, John looked nonplussed by her suggestion, and then he grinned.

'Nicely landed,' he acknowledged. 'I can't very well do otherwise now, can I? And it'll be an enormous feather in the cap of our little radio network, if it comes off.'

'Of course it'll come off. It's got to. Don't be such a

doubting Thomas. Even Mr Vyse was confident that it would be a success.'

Why did she have to bring the consultant's name into it again? Berry wondered vexedly. Julian Vyse's confidence was in himself, and in his own ability to make a success of whatever he chose to control. Clearly he intended to take control of her idea, unless she could prevent it.

Just as clearly, Berry intended to show him that she could do just as well, if not better, without his help.

She was denied the consolation of relieving her feelings into Trish's sympathetic ears on her way home afterwards. The ward sister was bearing down on a junior nurse who had a bundle of blankets in her arms, and a faraway look on her face.

'I said an extra pillow for the end bed, Nurse. Not an extra blanket.'

Trish raised her eyes heavenwards as the nurse scuttled away, red-faced, to change her armful.

'Young love,' the sister groaned. 'I shall be heartily thankful when the next few weeks are over.'

'Why the next few weeks?'

'By that time, the grapevine will have penetrated right through the hospital, and they'll have learned that Julian's a one-woman man, and not for them. Then, with a bit of luck, they'll stop mooning about, and give their attention to what I tell them again.'

A one-woman man. That meant Julian Vyse must be married. In spite of that, he had kissed her, Berry, as if he was thoroughly enjoying the experience.

He would not have the opportunity again, she vowed.

An anger as great as the anger she had felt against Chris choked Berry's throat as she digested the information. She had to substitute a wave of her hand for her usual cheerful 'goodnight' to Trish, because her vocal chords were too tight with temper to allow the words to come through.

What was it about her that made married men think they could use her for their own gratification, and get away with it? Chris had got away with it, but he was the first, and he would be the last.

If Julian Vyse tried to kiss her again, instead of his lips setting light to hers, he would find himself holding someone who was too hot to handle, she vowed fiercely.

# CHAPTER THREE

BERRY did not see the consultant in time to avoid him when she got to the hospital the next day.

She had already pressed the lift button, and was waiting without much confidence for the cage to appear, when Julian Vyse strolled across from casualty to wait beside her.

Berry shot him an unwelcoming look. Her immediate instinct was to abandon her wait and take to the stairs instead, but if she did it would make him think she was afraid of him, and in any case he might decide to walk upstairs with her.

The lift grumbled to a halt in front of her, and made up her mind. It caused her no surprise that it came, since Julian Vyse wanted it as well. Berry steeled her expression to one of cool indifference and stepped into the cage, and the consultant followed her.

He seemed to fill the lift. In spite of her outward cool, Berry felt nerves begin to flutter inside her stomach as he closed the gates, pressed the button, and remarked conversationally, 'Sister Connelly says your first name's Berry. It's unusual. Is it short for something?'

Taken aback by his unexpected question, Berry answered, 'My name's Rowan,' and resisted adding, 'though it's none of your business.'

'Berry suits you better,' he observed gravely.

'It'd suit me better if you'd pressed the right button,' she retorted as the lift shot straight past the floor she wanted. How typical of his arrogance that he had pressed the button for his own floor, without asking her first where she wanted to get out. 'Now I'll have to go back down again.'

'I'll take you, if you ask me nicely.'

In spite of yesterday, she did not expect him to kiss her in the lift, with the gates wide open on to the corridor, so she was unprepared when he barred her way through the gates, and drew her to him.

'Are you out of your mind?' She strained against his hold. 'If anyone sees us here, it'll be all over the hospital like wildfire. You must know what the grapevine's like in these places.'

If he made her the subject of gossip for the second time, she would never forgive him, she vowed angrily.

'Why does it bother you?' he murmured, his lips agonisingly close to her ear. They moved closer, and Berry felt her heart begin to thump.

If he heard it, he would know that he was the cause, and score another point over her. Berry struck out with words, because her arms were pinioned to her side, by the steel grip of his hands that held her still against him.

'You're one reason,' she flung. 'And your wife's the other. I don't flirt with married men.'

That made him release her. His hands dropped to his sides, but his eyes still held her, slit pinpoints of green as he ground out, 'My ... wife?'

'Don't tell me she doesn't understand you.'

Berry wondered fleetingly if anyone would ever be able fully to understand this self-contained creature, to whose face the dim light of the lift bulb had imparted a curious grey tinge. The silence between them seemed to stretch for ever, and his harsh tone made Berry jump when he broke it.

'It's a pity Trish Connelly doesn't subscribe to the grapevine, like the rest of the staff. But then, she never did gossip, or else you'd have learned by now that Kathleen, my wife, died.'

Pivoting on his heel, he strode away from Berry, along the corridor. She stared after him, too stunned to answer as he turned into his room and slammed the door after him.

Berry took her shock to Trish, with the excuse, 'I shan't be able to come in for a coffee later. We're all dining at the Vyse residence tonight, on orders from the great man himself.'

She tried to make her voice flippant, and she must have succeeded because Trish did not seem to notice anything amiss, simply replying casually, 'He's very lucky to have such a good housekeeper. He told me she came with him, from where he lived before.'

'Housekeeper?'

'Mmm. His wife died. He still carries a torch for her, though.'

'How?'

'She had a brain haemorrhage. Julian had to take the decision to switch off her life-support machine, poor lamb. He had to do the same thing the other night, for a young motor-cycle-accident victim. Imagine what it must be like, to have to do the same thing for someone else, when you've been through it all once yourself.'

Berry did not need to use her imagination. She had seen the effect written large on that strong, tormented face in the chapel.

Instead of arousing her sympathy, the knowledge she

had gleaned only served to fuel her anger against the consultant. Wolf would be a better description of him, she thought tartly.

If he was a one-woman man, as Trish said, and still carrying a torch for his dead wife, it meant that any other girls he kissed were merely scalps to him, to be collected in order to satisfy his ego.

It was a despicable thing to do, and Berry scrubbed her face with skin-grazing vigour to try to erase the impression his lips had left upon hers, as she got ready to go out that evening.

What did a chairperson dress in, to attend a campaign dinner? she wondered. She surveyed her wardrobe with brooding eyes. She needed something that would make her look taller, and older, and ... and ... invincible.

Not battle-axey. John was right. In spite of the new, tough outer shell she had grown round the old Berry, she could not change her real nature. But she needed some extra armour in order to be able to withstand her overbearing host. By inviting them all to dinner at his own house, Julian Vyse was, in effect, playing the match on his home ground.

The invitation of itself had wrested the initiative from out of her hands and into his, and Berry was determined that he should not be allowed to keep it there.

She wondered impatiently why her brainwave should have turned so unexpectedly into a duel of wills, since everyone at the dinner tonight would be motivated by the same charitable cause.

Human nature being what it was, she suspected shrewdly that the charity might not be so evident among some members of the cause's committee.

She flicked indecisively through her wardrobe.

She knew the dinner tonight would be crucial. Dinner was an inappropriate description. So far as she and Julian Vyse were concerned it would more probably turn out to be a meeting of the gladiators.

She found herself envying the two regular volunteers who would be taking over the studio in place of herself and John for this evening. They would probably have a far more peaceful time than themselves.

Eventually she decided upon a pale bronze, high-necked dress in watered silk, with a waist-length velvet cape in a deeper shade of the same colour, and lined with similar silk to that of her dress.

It picked out the glints in her hair, and the richly shaded material gave her slight figure a vivid glow. To Berry's dissatisfaction, it made her look not one day older.

Her only adornments were a gold rope necklet and a matching bracelet. She no longer wore her wedding-ring. A pair of high-heeled, strappy sandals increased her height and boosted her confidence, and when John and his wife picked her up just after seven o'clock Berry felt that she had done all she could in the way of armouring herself for the evening that lay ahead.

'Who else is coming?' John's wife asked, as Berry tucked herself into the back seat of the little red Metro and prepared to enjoy the unaccustomed treat of leaving the navigation to someone else. 'I meant to ask John, and forgot about it in the rush to get ready.'

'The mayor and his wife. Matron, and the hospital admin man. He's necesssary, because he'll have to be in on the discussions in order to get quotations for whatever medical equipment and so on is needed. Then there's yourself and John, of course. And me.'

Berry's voice trailed off. Belatedly, it dawned upon her that everyone else was neatly paired off, except for herself and her host. In the back of the car, her heart gave an uncomfortable lurch.

The last person she wanted to be paired off with was Julian Vyse, and she was thankful for the presence of the others to dilute the effect of his forceful personality.

The house stood some way out of the town, in about three acres of grounds, enjoyed a magnificent view of the harbour, and was in the most prestigious residential area of Aldermouth.

The building was long and low, and as the Metro drew to a halt in front of it Berry saw that it was made from warm-coloured stone. In the late evening sunshine it took on a drowsy, timeless look that did not reflect the abrasive character of its owner, she decided.

He was not in evidence to welcome them when they entered the spacious hall, and his white-haired housekeeper apologised on his behalf to the assembled guests.

'Mr Vyse has rung from the hospital, to say that he's been delayed, and would you mind not holding dinner for him? He'll be back just as soon as he can.'

All through the subsequent meal, Berry was acutely conscious of the vacant chair next to her own.

Her position against her host's seat would place her at his right hand, as his guest of honour, she realised, and decided that it must be in deference to her role as chairperson and not to herself as an individual.

It indicated just as clearly as if Julian Vyse had been there himself, and telling her in so many words, that he knew she would chair the committee, exactly as he had said she should.

Berry ground her teeth over his high-handed assumption, and picked at the delicious lobster starter on her plate with a nervy lack of appetite that was an insult to the speciality of Aldermouth's inshore fishing fleet.

She held a somewhat disjointed conversation with the mayoress, who sat on the left-hand side of the empty chair, which yawned between them like a silent reminder of the man who might return at any moment to occupy it.

The uncertainty of when that would be stretched Berry's already taut nerves as the meal progressed.

The food was sumptuous. It had been meticulously prepared and was faultlessly presented by a butler and uniformed maids, who were clearly trained to a very high standard of efficiency.

The exotic meal was in sharp contrast to the rest of the room, which was rather bare, Berry noticed, her eyes taking in the furnishings and décor interestedly.

She liked the lack of clutter, which added to the feeling of space, and accorded with her own taste. The room itself was large but, because the ceiling was not too high, its size was not oppressive.

The comparative scarcity of contents showed off to advantage the glorious colours of a hand-woven Persian carpet, bearing items of furniture so placed that there was sufficient room around each piece to be able to appreciate its individual beauty.

All the different English woods were present. Yew wood framed a china cabinet holding some exquisite pieces of porcelain, which Berry longed to examine more closely. A carved-oak sideboard glowed with years of loving polishing. A walnut writing-table stood to catch the light from the wide bay window, and surely the small, scattered stools were made of cherry wood?

Had Julian Vyse bought the house ready furnished, or had he chosen the pieces himself? Berry pondered. Or had he and his late wife chosen them together, lingering lovingly over each particular one, and now he cherished them for that reason?

She averted her eyes from the furniture as the door opened, and the subject of her thoughts apologised, 'I'm sorry to leave you on your own like this, but I was delayed by an emergency. It looks as if I'm just in time for pudding.'

He had taken the time to change, and his black and white dinner attire made him look even more attractive, and taller, if possible, than before.

'How far have you got with your discussions? Bring me up to date,' he bade Berry as he pulled out his chair, and sat down beside her.

'We haven't. I mean, we've been talking about other things.'

Generalities, Berry remembered vexedly. She had been so interested in taking stock of her surroundings that the reason for their being here had momentarily slipped to the back of her mind.

In spite of herself, she had become preoccupied in trying to read the room as a clue to the elusive character of its owner, that character that he managed to keep so effectively shuttered behind the twin barriers of those cool green eyes.

'We've been waiting for you to arrive, Mr Vyse,' the mayor's wife put in with a smile and, returning it, her host said to his guests at large,

'Don't you think, as we'll all be working together, we could drop the formalities? My name's Julian.'

The concession did nothing to detract from his calm

assumption of control, Berry noticed, and knew angrily that they had all, unconsciously, been putting off the discussion until Julian arrived. Waiting like sheep for him to take the lead, she mentally belaboured herself and them.

As chairperson, she should have grasped that lead firmly in her own hands, and turned the leisurely meal into a working dinner, and she saw now, too late, that she had allowed a golden opportunity to slip through her fingers.

What a triumph it would have been, if she had used the time to beat out a concrete plan of action, ready to put in front of Julian as a *fait accompli* the moment he came in.

Instead, she had allowed herself to be distracted, but with a confident tilt of her chin she told him, 'It saves time going over every item twice, if we're all in on the discussions together.'

She tried to make it look as if the omission was deliberate policy on her part, instead of time wasted, but realised frustratedly, from the green glance he slanted at her, that her explanation cut no ice with him.

She watched vexedly as Julian gathered the committee into his own competent grasp with a crisp, 'In that case, shall we take coffee in the drawing-room, and start our discussions right away?'

He forced the pace of the subsequent talk with a remorseless energy that set at nought the long and exhausting day he must have endured at the hospital, and made Berry glad of the excellent coffee as a booster to her own flagging energies.

Even the mayor, she noticed irritably, conceded leadership to the consultant, although fairness made

Berry excuse him, on the grounds that, where the needs of the hospital were concerned, Julian must be the acknowledged expert in his own field.

Whether he was or not, she suspected he would have taken the lead as his inalienable right, and resentment at his high-handedness grew in her as the evening progressed.

Various schemes were put forward to raise money. The usual dances, raffles, jumble sales and coffee mornings were suggested and agreed, and Julian concurred readily with each one. But, covertly watching him, Berry noticed a reservation in his expression which gave her an uneasy feeling that he might have other and very different ideas of his own, which he intended to force through once the scheme got under way.

What those ideas might be she could not begin to guess, but she had to admit that Julian's energy was infectious. He transmitted his own sense of urgency to them all, like a shot in the arm.

'The emergency that delayed me tonight——' he began, and gained immediate attention from his listeners. He sat forward in his chair, his coffee forgotten and growing cold on the table beside him, and his lean face was tight with the memory of the things he had seen, and had to cope with tonight.

'Tell us what happened, Julian,' John prompted.

'It was a street accident, involving two children. They've had to be placed in general surgical. Sister Connelly already has several children there, and two more is two too many in an adult ward.'

Berry sprang to the defence of her friend. 'Sister Connelly is more than capable of coping, however many children you have to send her.'

'All the nursing staff are capable of coping. But children need special attention.'

'They'll get the very best from Trish.'

'Even so, children need nurses hand-picked, and specially trained to look after them alone. They also need sufficient nurses, with enough time to spare to sit on the end of their cots and read them a story. Time to lift them out of their cots now and then, and give them a cuddle to help them over the bad spots.'

Berry stared at him, startled. Underneath his tough exterior, Julian was revealing an unexpectedly sensitive side that she suspected few people ever saw.

He went on swiftly, as if he sensed her surprise, and drew an instant curtain over whatever softer side of his nature was there, which he did not intend to show.

'What if there had been twenty children, instead of just two? What if, say, a school bus had crashed, instead of it being just two individual little boys, who were victims of their own reckless game of do-or-dare with the traffic at the intersection? How would St Luke's have coped then?'

St Luke's would not, and they all knew it.

'We've never had an accident on that scale before,' the hospital admin man ventured, and was instantly silenced by a frosty look from Julian.

'Because there hasn't been one yet, it isn't to say that it won't happen in the future. With the growth of the holiday industry, Aldermouth is coping with an influx of traffic such as it's never experienced before. It's no use waiting for an emergency to happen before getting geared up to cope with it.'

'I've had some posters roughed out, and I've brought them along to see what you think of them.' Tactfully, the mayor smoothed over the slight contretemps, and then lowered himself in Berry's eyes by handing the posters first of all to Julian.

'These two are excellent.' The consultant gave the pack a swift glance, and extracted two sheets, without first passing them all round for a general opinion.

Berry's lips tightened. 'I'd like to see the posters as well, please.' She held out her hand for them determinedly.

'Of course.' Julian handed her the two he had chosen.

'*All* of them,' Berry insisted. 'It's for the whole committee to decide on what publicity we use.' Not just you, she added as a silent rider.

Hazel eyes, and narrowed green, measured each other across the fan of papers still in Julian's hand. Something flashed deep in the green, but wordlessly their owner placed the rest of the posters in Berry's grasp, and she lowered her eyes to look at them, conscious that her heart was beating uncomfortably fast with the tension of the confrontation.

She had won her point, but not, she knew angrily, the whole round. She saw at once that the two posters Julian had chosen were far superior to the others.

The messages carried by both of them were instantly eye-catching and served their purpose admirably but, refusing to be defeated, she shuffled all the sheets together, making sure that the two Julian had chosen were lost in the pack, before she passed them round, determined that the other members of the committee should not be influenced.

Julian threw her an oblique look when the general consensus agreed his choice, and smarting, Berry had reluctantly to cast her vote in line with the rest.

'That settles it.' Julian handed the pack back to the mayor. 'How soon can you have a quantity printed, ready for distribution?'

'By mid-morning tomorrow. I'm tied up on civic duties for the rest of the day, but I'll try to find someone to take at least a few of them round.'

'I'll help,' Berry offered readily. 'I'm going to the hospital to measure up the rooms first thing in the morning, but when I've done that I'll be free until it's time for the evening broadcast.'

'John and I will do some for you,' the producer's wife added, and Julian cut in with,

'We'll split the town in two between us. Berry and I will take the north side, if you'll take the south, John?'

The town was cleanly divided by the river Alder, and would be more efficiently covered that way, but ... Berry and I?

Berry caught a sharp breath. 'I shan't be free until mid-morning,' she countered quickly. 'You go ahead on your own.'

How dared Julian try to control where she should distribute her leaflets, and presume to partner her, to boot, without even having the decency to ask first if she minded?

'Mid-morning is when the posters will be ready, and the quicker they're put up, the quicker we'll get a response to our appeal.'

Julian cut across Berry's attempt to protest, and swept on, 'We shall get the job done in half the time if we work in tandem. One can take one side of a street, and one the other. If we work single-handed, it will mean retracing our steps, and take twice as long.'

He was quite right, of course. Berry bit her lip, but

before she could think up another excuse, Julian added,

'I want to be at the hospital early myself, to check on the two children who had the accident this evening. I'll meet you there. If I'm in time, I'll give you a hand with the measuring up.'

Not if she could help it, Berry vowed. She would get to the hospital very early, hurry up with her measuring, and slip away before Julian arrived.

The mayor rose to his feet.

'That seems to be all we can do for the moment. I suggest we all meet again later to check on progress. In the meantime, we'll go away and leave you to get some rest, Julian. It must have been a long day for you.'

It had been a long day for them all but, unlike his guests, Julian had missed most of his dinner, and had expended any surplus energy he might have had left on forcing the pace of the meeting in a manner that left Berry, for one, feeling breathless.

Their host could relax when they had all gone home, she thought sourly. Laden bookshelves, and a Bechstein grand, were pointers to the way in which he might spend any scarce leisure hours. But perhaps they had belonged to Kathleen, and not to him?

Sudden dejection caught at her, probably occasioned by the growing hour, and her own busy day. A bustle ensued, of coats being brought and distributed, and Berry reached for her cape, but Julian's hand forestalled her.

'Let me help you,' he said, picking it up and slipping it across her shoulders. 'Velvet becomes you,' he opined, and smoothed his sensitive surgeon's fingers across the soft, pale bronze pile.

His touch made Berry's skin prickle, as if tiny electric

shocks followed the course of his hand across her shoulders. She blamed the static electricity in the material, and shrugged away the goose-pimples that sent a shiver to follow the prickles.

'Are you cold?' He picked up the tremor immediately, and his hands came round to fix the clasp of the cape across her throat. He had to stoop slightly to do it, and his fingers came up under her chin, and tipped up her face in order to give himself more room to manoeuvre.

'Keep your chin up,' he bade her. 'I can't see properly, otherwise, to fix this buckle.'

Bending down brought his eyes on a level with her own, and Berry gave a convulsive swallow as she met their full dynamic force at close range. His fingers brushed against her neck as they fumbled with the delicate clasp, and the tingles that had afflicted her shoulders moments before seemed to paralyse her throat muscles now.

This time, there was no material between them, so static electricity could not be to blame, although electricity of a different kind seemed to crackle from his finger-ends to burn her tender skin, and the word 'lightning' flashed unheralded across Berry's mind.

A lightning bolt was what it felt like, to be touched by Julian.

It took mere seconds for him to close the clasp of her cape, but they seemed to stretch into an eternity before he released her, stepped back, and remarked casually, 'That'll keep out the cold when you go outside.'

His touch had brought a heat to her cheeks that made Berry long to toss aside the cape, but the possibility that Julian would help her on with it again stayed her hand. Instead she lifted her face to the blessed freshness of the night air, in order to bring her cheeks back to their more accustomed colour.

'Goodnight, and thank you for the dinner. It's been a delightful evening.' The mayor shook hands heartily with his host, and Julian turned and bent over the hand of the mayoress with an old-world courtesy that seemed entirely natural with him, and had no hint in it of the theatrical.

The mayor turned to his car, which for such informal occasions was his own small family saloon and self-driven, and he was about to insert his key in the door lock when he looked down, and gave an irate exclamation, 'Confound it! I've got a flat tyre.'

He stared ruefully at the front off-side wheel, which was collapsed in sad resignation on to the gravel below it.

'I'm afraid I shall have to ring for a taxi to take us home, Julian. Do you mind if I use your phone?'

'If there was room in the Metro, I'd offer to take you,' John said regretfully. 'Your house is on our side of the town.'

'Then why not take them, and I'll take Berry home?' Julian put in instantly.

Ignoring Berry's hasty, 'I wouldn't dream of troubling you,' he ushered the mayor and his wife into John's car.

He turned back to Berry. 'Go back indoors for a while, out of the chill, while I get my car out.'

Why had she not come in her own, instead of being tempted by John's kindly offer of a lift? Berry said stiffly, 'Really, Mr Vyse, there's no need. I can quite easily take a taxi.'

'I thought we agreed, my name is Julian?'

'Julian, then.' Berry shifted uneasily from one foot to

the other. 'Really, I'd much rather take a taxi. It isn't very far.'

'Have you got a piece of gravel in your shoe?'

'No ... yes.' The unexpectedness of the question startled her. It also warned her that this man's eyes missed nothing, and to cover her confusion Berry bent and pretended to extract a non-existent piece of gravel from her sandal.

'I wouldn't dream of allowing you to return home unescorted,' he said.

'I always return home unescorted from the studio at night, much later than this.'

'But not when you're my guest. Go inside, while I get the car out of the garage.'

His tone brooked no refusal, and reluctantly Berry retraced her steps to the drawing-room. She could hardly commandeer his telephone against his wishes, but her independent spirit rebelled against his arrogant authority.

He always managed to dredge up an excellent reason for having his own way, but that did nothing to sweeten the medicine he doled out, and in Berry's mouth it tasted distinctly sour. Restlessly, she prowled the carpet, until she heard the front door shut again, and firm footsteps return along the hall.

She tensed as Julian reappeared outside the drawing-room door, but instead of coming straight through he stepped to one side to allow his housekeeper to precede him into the room.

'I've brought you a pot of coffee and some sandwiches, Mr Vyse, because you missed your dinner. The caterers have gone, and ... oh, I'm sorry, sir. I thought your guests had all left.' The elderly woman espied

Berry for the first time.

'The mayor's car had a flat tyre, so he's left it here until the morning. He and his wife doubled up in the other car, and I'm taking Miss Baker home.'

'In that case, sir, would you like me to bring in another cup? There's plenty of coffee, and the young lady might like a warm drink before you start out.'

'That's an excellent idea, Mrs Morgan. Thank you.'

Julian's smile was warm and wide and relaxed, as the housekeeper went on her self-imposed mission, and it riveted Berry's attention. She had wondered what it would be like to see him really smile, and now she knew. It sent an odd feeling shafting through her that she was at a loss to explain.

It was the smile of a man who had shut the world outside, and was at peace in his own surroundings. As if, with the departure of his guests, he need no longer call upon the dynamic driving-force that made him such a dominant figure during his working day.

As if, Berry thought with rising wrath, she herself was so insignificant in his eyes that he thought any driving force was unnecessary when he was in her company.

The housekeeper returned with the extra cup, and Julian dismissed her with a smile of thanks, and said to Berry, 'Will you be mother?'

Without thinking, she justified his humiliating assumption by picking up the pot to pour out, and immediately wished she had not.

But it was too late, the cup was rapidly filling and, when Julian put up his hand to indicate that that was enough, she had no option but to obey his imperious signal, and stop pouring, or the dark aromatic liquid would have spilled over the cup's rim.

Berry enjoyed coffee. She would doubtless have
brewed some for herself when she got home, but she did
not want this particular cupful now.

She refused Julian's offer of a sandwich, and perched
uneasily on the edge of her chair, wondering how long it
would be before he finished his own drink, and
condescended to take her home.

These days she was accustomed to driving her own car
and was not used to waiting on other people's
convenience, and it went against the grain, especially
with Julian.

The silence in the room seemed to wrap itself round
them, made deeper by the ticking of the mother-of-pearl
inlaid long-case clock standing in a corner of the room.

Julian spoke into the void, and Berry's coffee gave a
dangerous lurch to the rim of her cup as his deep voice
cut into her consciousness.

'Were you wondering why I had caterers to do the
dinner tonight?' he asked.

He had a penchant for asking unexpected questions. A
disconcerting one, Berry found, that had a habit of
catching her unawares, and leaving her searching for an
answer, when she would fain have found a swift and
telling retort that would show this overpowering man
she was not a pawn to be pushed around in whichever
direction he chose.

'No. Why should I? Your domestic arrangements are
nothing to do with me.'

Berry made her voice sound uninterested, but she
admitted to herself privately that the discovery had
caused her some surprise. She had assumed that the
uniformed staff were part of Julian's household.

'Engaging a caterer saves having to eat up a lot of

leftovers after a dinner party.'

He smiled amusedly, that warm, full, all-embracing smile that did astonishing things to his face, and Berry felt her heart give a lurch to imitate the coffee in her cup.

'How sensible,' was all she could find to say.

'It saves Mrs Morgan a good deal of hard work and hassle. It isn't fair to expect her to cope with dinner parties, at her age.'

Again, that unexpected touch of thoughtfulness. Reluctantly, Berry ticked up one more point in his favour. She gave him a curious look, and was unnerved to find him watching her.

She lowered her eyes hastily to her cup, and wished that he would get on with his coffee instead of talking. She felt acutely conscious of their isolation in this silent room, and oddly vulnerable now that the others had left.

Julian sipped his drink slowly, savouring its flavour with the appreciation of a man who is abstemious with food and drink, and yet extracts the full enjoyment from both.

Berry decided on drastic action to cut short his enjoyment of this particular drink. Nervily, she wondered what topic of conversation he might broach next, if they remained in this unwelcome tête-à-tête situation, sure only that, whatever it was, Julian would remain in firm control, and steer it in which ever direction he might please, whether she herself wanted it to go that way or not.

Remembering her gaffe when she'd been with Trish, Berry decided she did not. Goaded by uncertainty, she deliberately raised her fingers to her lips to cover a wholly manufactured yawn.

Her ploy worked. Instantly, Julian put down his cup,

still only half finished, Berry noticed, and contrarily felt guilty at cutting short his much needed refreshment.

'You're sleepy,' he observed. 'If you've had enough coffee, let's go.'

'Finish your own first.' Belated compunction forced Berry to retract, but he shook his head.

'I'll have some more when I come back. Don't worry,' as she was about to protest further, 'the pot's a Thermos. The coffee will be just as hot when I get back as it is now. Mrs Morgan often leaves me a snack if I'm delayed at the hospital and have to miss a meal. This way, it saves her having to wait round to brew a fresh drink when I do turn up.'

One more evidence of his thoughtfulness, which made Berry instantly feel worse. Torn between an increasing sense of guilt and anger at herself for feeling that way, she followed Julian out of the house to where his car was drawn up beside the front door.

It was a Jaguar. Long and low and sleek, with the same appearance of leashed power in its classic lines as its owner.

Julian helped her into the front passenger seat and, bending down, he carefully tucked her dress out of the way of the door, giving her a close view of his cleanly barbered nape, into which the deep auburn waves of his hair rolled with neat precision.

Berry's fingertips knew a rebel urge to dip themselves in the waves, and sternly she clasped them into submission under her cape as he shut the door and came to join her behind the wheel. She relaxed into the luxurious upholstery as the car engine purred into life, and the powerful headlights guided the long bonnet down the drive.

Julian was silent as he drove, concentrating on guiding the big car smoothly along the narrow twisting lanes, but Berry had plenty to occupy her mind, as through the darkness her own heightened senses talked to her instead.

Subtle messages reached her. The crunch of hide upholstery caught her ears as Julian moved slightly in his seat to manipulate the car controls.

A faint whiff of expensive aftershave lotion was tantalisingly wafted by the movement to her small snub nose, and her pulse accelerated, stung into quickened life by the sensuous mixture of spices, which that *retroussé* organ sped to her every tingling nerve.

Lights invaded the car as they neared the town, and Berry felt irrationally glad of their illumination in the car, to dilute the disturbing vibes as Julian reduced his speed cautiously to negotiate the still narrow but more populated streets.

People spilled out of a tavern doorway and wandered heedlessly across the street, oblivious of their near extinction, and Julian slammed his foot down on the brake, bringing the Jaguar to a rocking halt. His swift glance across at Berry vindicated his decision to bring her home himself, but his only comment was a dry, 'At this rate, we might need another adult ward, as well.'

He did not speak again until they reached the end of Berry's street. John must have given him her address, she surmised. She did not remember doing so herself. But, for all that he was a comparative newcomer to the town, Julian seemed to have a remarkable sense of direction, or perhaps he had studied a town map and discovered where she lived first, because he turned the car unerringly into the small cul-de-sac off the street proper, which housed the tall, old-fashioned villas that had been converted into such roomy flats.

He stopped in front of her flat without, she noticed, having first to crawl the car to look for the house number, but before surprise had time to register, he was out of the tidily parked Jaguar and opening the passenger door to help her to alight.

His hand steadied her as she swung her legs out of the car and manoeuvred herself on to her high heels from the deep well of the seat that seemed reluctant to let her go.

Julian drew Berry up to stand in front of him, uncomfortably close. She backed off a step, hurriedly, intending to part company with him there and then on the pavement.

Formal words of thanks for the evening, and the lift home, rose to her lips, but before she could utter them Julian insisted, 'I'll see you inside.' As if he would not feel satisfied until he had seen her through the safety of her own front door.

He walked her determinedly up the short flight of steps and into the deep, shadowy lobby, and Berry's heart missed a beat as he took her front-door key from her fingers. Did he expect her to invite him inside, now he had brought her home?

Did he intend to come inside with her, whether she invited him or not?

He seemed to be in no greater hurry to leave her than he had been to finish his coffee earlier. He said, and his deep voice sent an answering quiver across Berry's taut nerves, 'We'll be meeting a good deal, from now on.'

'We shall *all* be meeting, until the ward is opened and paid for.'

Hastily, Berry depersonalised any future meetings, and again that hint of a smile, mocking her now, touched the well cut lips.

'As head of the committee, you'll have lots to do.'

Berry shot him a wary look. He had pushed her into doing the job. Was he taunting her now, because of the heavy workload which he had forced willy-nilly on to her slight shoulders? She stiffened them, and her chin rose.

'I've decided to share the chair with John. We'll halve the work between us. Matron and the mayor will both have help from their own staff.'

It was *her* decision to split the job, not Julian's, and he should see that she was not prepared to come begging to him for any help she herself might need.

'You make a far more decorative chairperson than John.'

The cheek of the man! Berry flashed, 'I'm in the chair to work, not to be a decoration.'

No one had ever called her decorative before. Cute, yes. Gorgeous. That was Chris. She discarded his fulsome compliments for what they were worth.

Berry had one word for her own face. Ordinary. At boarding-school, the old-fashioned headmistress discouraged what she regarded as vanity, and all that went with it, including make-up.

As a result, Berry had grown up with an unjustifiably low opinion of her own dainty loveliness, and a fine, clear skin that was unspoiled by early make-up, and which still only received a hasty dab of powder now and then when she was going out.

Decorative. She savoured the word. The odd compliment gave her a distinctly odd feeling. Royal Doulton figurines were decorative. But so was icing on a cake, which had the added advantage of being sweet to taste.

Deep in conjecture, Berry was caught unaware as Julian's head bent low over her, and his lips came down to taste the sweetness of her mouth.

Her mind went blank as he drew her to him, and his mouth covered hers with a seeking pressure that sent sudden wild sensations flooding through her.

The force of it took her completely by surprise. It carried her along with it at a dizzy pace that gave her no time to think, no time to act, only to feel, and set at nought the speed of the committee proceedings which Julian had pressured earlier on.

Desperately Berry fought against the flood. Julian was scalp-hunting, and hers was not for the taking. He was a one-woman man. That was what Trish had said. A one-woman man, and that woman was Kathleen, his dead wife.

The name dammed the flood as if it had come up against a solid wall, but its waves left a savage turbulence inside Berry that threatened to engulf her. Desperately, she struck out to keep herself afloat, striking at Julian, pushing him away from her with arms that gained a sudden frantic strength.

Her lips were parted, throbbing with the feel of his kiss. Her breath panted as if she had been running, and when Julian held her at arm's length, she stared up at him with wild eyes.

'What on earth's the matter?' He stared at her impatiently. 'Are you a man-hater, or something? Surely you're not one of these ultra-liberated types, who's decided to dispense with men? Or have you had a love affair that's gone wrong? Is that it? It happens to us all, in one way or another.'

Obliquely he was referring to his dead wife, but Berry brushed the reference aside.

'If I've decided to dispense with men, the reason's got nothing to do with you.'

She wrenched herself free from his hold and fled through the front door and up the stairs as if her feet had wings, leaving the key still in the lock, and Julian standing below in the darkened lobby, watching her precipitate flight.

She was out of breath, and her heart thumped painfully as she gained her flat, and heard the street door shut with that peculiar 'crump' of sticking wood that made such an excellent warning of an impending visitor.

She strained her ears until it felt as if the drums must surely burst, listening for the sound of footsteps following her up the stairs; but none came, and seconds later a metallic clank from the tiled hall below told her that Julian must have pushed her key through the letter box, for her to retrieve at her leisure.

Moments later, the faint purr of a car engine split the silence of the cul-de-sac, and without switching on the light Berry ran to the window, pushed back the curtain and watched as the Jaguar nosed its way back to the main road and disappeared into the night.

Long after it had gone, she remained leaning on the windowsill. Her whole body trembled with reaction. Since Chris, she had avoided all social contact with men, and that was the way she wanted it to stay, she told herself fiercely. Her work she could cope with, but nothing more.

And now, out of the blue, just when she was regaining her lost confidence, and getting her life organised to her liking, this arrogant, dictatorial, overwhelming senior consultant at St Luke's had gate-crashed through the barrier she had so carefully erected round herself.

If he had the nerve to try again, he would find that barrier reinforced with stouter material than he bargained for, she vowed.

If Julian was a one-woman man, in another sense she, Berry, was a one-man woman. One man had been more than enough so far as she was concerned, and it was a mistake she did not intend to make again.

So why should she feel this lingering sense of letdown, that Julian had contented himself with dropping her key through the letterbox, for her to find and pick up for herself, instead of following her upstairs to her flat to give it to her in person?

# CHAPTER FOUR

THE alarm bell sent out a shrill summons. Berry stirred drowsily. Seven o'clock. It was Saturday, so there was no need to rush.

And then she remembered. If she was to give Julian the slip, as she'd planned, she would have to be at St Luke's very early, and be finished with her measuring up before he had time to leave his patients and join her.

A pair of spiky-heeled sandals lying where she had kicked them off the night before were a sharp reminder, if she needed one, of Julian's attempted takeover of the rest of her Saturday.

'We'll see about that,' Berry promised herself grimly, and padded into the kitchen to make herself a reviving cup of coffee.

Half an hour later, she was showered and dressed in a workmanlike outfit of flat, soft-soled shoes, suitable for her energetic morning, topped by tan-coloured slacks and a matching high-necked sweater.

The flat-heeled slip-ons brought her down to her usual diminutive height, but it could not be helped, and since she intended to be out of St Luke's before Julian got there it did not matter.

Armed with a shoulder-bag bulging with measuring gear, notebooks and pens, she bestirred her car from its garage, and set off through the unaccustomed quiet of the weekend streets.

Although it was still very early, Julian had a habit of doing the unexpected, and Berry warily avoided the usual entrance which might bring her on a collision course with the consultant when she was leaving, and went in by a back entrance instead, depositing her car in another park at the rear of the building.

The wing towards which she was heading had been closed for so long that the porter had some difficulty in finding the right key, and Berry fidgeted uneasily while he consulted his record book to make sure he had the right number, but when she reached her goal the key fitted, and she let herself into the empty rooms with a feeling that she had successfully run the gauntlet so far.

The rooms did not appear at first sight to be in such a dilapidated condition as Trish's gloomy predictions had led her to expect. They were empty, except for a long-forgotten patient-trolley parked in one corner, and a check with the hospital electrician confirmed that the wiring was in a safe working condition, which left only the decorations to be dealt with.

Berry got out her measuring-tape and notebook and set to work. Assessment of the purely cosmetic needs of the room should not take too long, and with a bit of luck she would be finished and away again before Julian even arrived at the hospital.

Time fled. She tackled the playroom first, which was the room the consultant wanted to put into use right away. The kindly electrician lent her a lightweight step-ladder, and left her to it.

She was lost in contemplation of whether to use curtains or blinds at the large windows when a voice spoke from immediately underneath her feet.

'Do you want me to hold one end of the measuring-tape for you?'

'For goodness' sake . . .'

The step-ladder rocked precariously as Berry spun

round, and Julian grabbed at it to prevent it from tipping her off the top.

'Have a care, or you'll be the first patient in the new ward.'

'The ward's supposed to be for children, not for adults.' Her voice was sharp with the fright he had given her.

'From where I'm standing, you don't look much older than ...'

From where she was standing, Julian looked ... Berry swallowed suddenly. The consultant was in mufti this morning, and the elegantly casual clothes changed his appearance completely.

His hair shone like burnished copper against the natural-coloured roll-neck cashmere sweater, topping dark jade-green trousers and suede slip-on shoes in the same soft shade.

But underneath the deceptive attire still lurked the same Julian, Berry reminded herself, and the knowledge edged her voice as she retorted, 'I'm twenty-three, no matter what I happen to look like. And you should know better than to creep up on people like that.'

He had caught up with her in spite of her precautions, and Berry did not know whether to be angrier with herself or with him. Most of the human race would still be occupied with their Saturday breakfasts, so why could he not behave like one of them?

Her experience so far of his energetic drive gave her the answer. Her heart thudded. It was the fright he had given her, she told herself crossly, and flared her vexation from her elevated perch.

It made her feel good to be looking down at Julian, instead of having to crane her neck to look up at him, and she took full advantage of her position while it lasted.

'It's dangerous to make people jump like that. You nearly made me fall off the ladder. I thought you said you'd got enough patients, without inviting any more.'

'I spoke to you when I came through the door, but you were lost in thought at the window.'

'I was weighing up the advantages of using curtains or blinds.'

'Blinds,' Julian decided for her instantly, and Berry's hackles rose. What she had been afraid of was happening. He had not been in the room for two minutes and he was taking charge again!

'Curtains are cosier,' she contradicted him instantly. 'This is the playroom, not the ward.'

'It's the playroom to serve the ward. It needs to be bright and cheerful, but hygiene has to be the first consideration, and long curtains harbour dust. In a hospital situation, that means germs.'

His argument was unassailable, as were all his comments on almost every aspect of the job Berry touched on. He followed her round the rooms, altering every suggestion she made, no matter how slight, until she could have screamed her frustration.

The worst part of it was that he was so right about everything.

Berry's experience of decorating so far had been confined to a purely domestic situation, and in a hospital environment she discovered that there were all sorts of comparatively minor things to be taken into account, such as glare from high-gloss paintwork that might bring discomfort to small eye-sufferers on a bright sunny day, which would not have occurred to her until Julian pointed it out.

From his privileged position, he knew what snags to look out for, and Berry learned fast, but it rasped at her pride that it should be the consultant who was doing the teaching.

Feeling his eyes upon her, she looked up, and knew that the narrowed pinpoints of speculating green read her rebellious thoughts and scorned them.

'My only interest is in the welfare of the children,' he told her curtly, and Berry flushed resentfully at his tone.

Whatever his interest in his small patients, there was absolutely no justification for him to roller-coaster over other people's feelings in quite such an abrasive manner in order to achieve his ends.

'So is mine,' she declared hotly.

'In that case, act on another of my suggestions. To please me,' he added as he saw her hesitate.

'Suggestions? They sound more like orders to me.' She did not particularly want to please him, and the desire to do so was growing less by the minute.

His shrug dismissed her complaint as petty. 'Call them what you like, but at least listen. This one will be more difficult than the others. Out of the ordinary.'

'I'm quite capable of dealing with something that's out of the ordinary.'

Did he imagine she was only capable of coping with mundane things like church jumble sales?

'You mentioned putting nursery cutouts along the walls of the ward and the playroom.'

'You agreed it would be a good idea.' Surely there was nothing he could find to object to in nursery cutouts?

'So it is. In the ward, put some on the ceiling, as well.'

'Eh?' Berry stared. 'Frescoed ceilings are going a bit far in a hospital ward, surely?'

He must be joking. They could not afford to waste

money on flights of fancy. Berry's nerves, ragged at the end of the tense session of suggestion and counter-suggestion, were not inclined to see the funny side.

'Not frescoes. Nursery cut-outs. Something the children will be familiar with from their story books.'

'OK, nursery cut-outs. But why on the ceiling, for goodness' sake?'

Trust Julian to latch on to the one item of decorating that had, up to now, defeated her. She would have to beg the help of someone from the maintenance department to cope with the ceiling, she decided, but she refused to allow her reservation to show in front of Julian.

Instead of answering her question, he reached out and drew the patient-trolley towards them.

'Lie down on that,' he told her.

This was going too far. 'Joke over,' Berry refused sharply. 'Lie down on it yourself if you want to. Why should I?'

'I'm not joking, Berry. I'm trying to get a point over to you. Do as I say.'

Berry eyed him frostily. Was he trying to make a fool of her?

'Please, Berry. It's important.'

'Oh, well, if I must.' She eyed the trolley with open distaste. 'It's too high for me to get on,' she discovered thankfully.

'That's no problem.'

Before she could prevent him, Julian bent down and swung her up in his arms as if she were indeed, no more than a child. For a palpitating moment, Berry found herself suspended just under his chin.

There was just the faintest hint of a cleft in it, she discovered, and felt a peculiar sensation shaft right through her as his arms tightened round her, cradling her so closely to him that she could smell the now familiar scent of his aftershave lotion.

She gave an embarrassed wriggle, and he looked down into her upturned face, a long, considering look that momentarily stilled her wriggle, and almost her breath along with it, before he released her gently on to the trolley and asked her—not ordered, she noticed, surprised—but asked her, to lie down.

The change in tone did what an order could not, and Berry reluctantly complied. At once, Julian spoke, and again it was an order.

'Now you're lying flat, look up at the ceiling.' She did so, too surprised not to, and he asked, 'What do you see?'

'A white ceiling.' What did he expect her to see? The stars?

'Exactly. Boring, isn't it?'

'You mean ...?' Enlightenment began to dawn.

'I mean, that children who for one reason or another are obliged to lie flat on their backs, and may not always be well enough to read or to play with their toys, have nothing on which to feed their imaginations. Pictures on the ceiling could relieve many an hour's boredom for such youngsters.'

'It's a marvellous idea! I'd never have thought of such a thing myself,' Berry had to confess.

'You've obviously never been a child in hospital.'

'No, I haven't.'

Had Julian, she wondered? If he had not, he was showing an unusual degree of perception in putting himself in the position of the children in his care.

If he had ... The thought of her companion as a small boy in hospital, perhaps in pain, or homesick, gave Berry's heart a curious twist. Abruptly, she thrust it aside and began to pull herself upright on the trolley.

'Bear with me for another minute.'

Instantly, Julian's hand came down on her shoulder, pressing her prone again, and Berry knew a dreadful feeling of helplessness as he kept his hand where it was to prevent her from rising, and wheeled her to the side of the ward, to the place where eventually a cot would stand.

Settling the trolley to his satisfaction, he hunkered down beside it, and brought his eyes on a level with her own, so close that if there had been a pillow on the trolley his head would have rested on it beside her.

Confusion made Berry's pulse race, and she felt thankful that Julian's hand was on her shoulder and not on her wrist, so that he could have no conception of the effect he was having upon her. Nervously, her eyes followed his pointing finger towards the ceiling.

'When you fix your pictures up there, remember to place them in a way that they don't look upside down to the patient. It'll mean doing two friezes, one to face each side of the ward. Children have got a large bump of curiosity, and it's frustrating not to be able to see a picture clearly, so remember to tell whoever puts them up there not to scatter them haphazardly, so that a child has to twist round in order to see what the pictures are. Do you see what I mean?'

He turned his head to make sure that she saw, and at the same time Berry turned hers on the trolley, and their eyes met, and instead of nursery cut-outs, Berry's eyes encountered green fire.

She tried to pull her head back, but the trolley was below her, preventing any movement in that direction. His hand on her shoulder held her prone, and Berry felt herself go rigid as his breath fanned her cheek.

Her world became circumscribed by emerald stars,

circled by an auburn sun. They hovered over her, closing in on her. Her bemused mind had only time to grasp the fact that the sun and stars were at different ends of the day, when the crescent moon of his smiling lips descended to meet her own.

The contact sent Berry's senses into a total eclipse that made the world vanish behind Julian's shadow, and only awareness of him remained, sending shooting stars zinging through her mind in a dazzling explosion that sent her leaping pulses into orbit.

'Miss Baker? Have you finished with my steps?'

The electrician! Berry crashed to earth. With frantic hands, she pushed Julian away from her, pushed herself upright, and stared in total dismay at the grinning face which was poking round the ward doorway.

'Sorry to disturb you, love, but there's a light fitting gone on the blink in one of the wards, and I need my steps to fix it.'

The blue-overalled figure was not sorry at all. His interested eyes took in Berry's tumbled hair, her scarlet cheeks, and her awful, compromising, totally misleading position on the trolley.

They drew erroneous conclusions from what they saw, and made them plain in the electrician's parting shot as he shouldered his steps with a laughing. 'As you were, both,' and emphasised what he thought by slamming the door ostentatiously behind him.

The man's duties took him to every corner of the hospital, Berry knew, and he was by far the biggest gossip of any member of staff.

'Get me off this thing!' Recklessly, she swung her legs clear of the trolley.

'Have a care, or you'll fall.'

Julian grabbed her round the waist with both hands as

the trolley wheels rolled under her convulsive movement, and the next moment she was on her feet and
facing him, glaring up into his amused face.

Amused, at her expense.

'It's nothing to laugh about,' she cried. 'The
electrician's version of what he saw will be all over the
hospital, quicker than if I broadcast it myself on the
radio.'

'Why should you let gossip on the grapevine worry
you? If you work in a closed community, you're bound
to be the subject of it at some time or another, whether
you like it or not.'

'I don't like it. No one will ever believe the real reason
why I was on that trolley, and you know it. Thanks to
you, my name will be mud throughout the hospital for
weeks to come.'

'You're your own person. You don't have to justify
your actions to anyone. It'll be a nine-days' wonder,
until the next thing crops up to take their attention.'

He was right again, but Berry was in no mood to listen
to platitudes. She knew she was over-sensitive on the
subject of gossip, but the old adage of 'once bitten, twice
shy' applied, and she smarted at being in that same
position again, not least because it was Julian who put
her there.

'Mud sticks.'

If his kisses had been genuine, it might not have
seemed so bad, but the knowlege that he was only using
her, to try to add another scalp to his doubtless already
overloaded belt, rubbed salt into Berry's lacerated pride.

'Forget it,' Julian said impatiently. 'Let's go and get
the Jag, and collect our posters from the town hall.'

'I've got my own car here. I'll go in that.'

Right now, Berry wanted nothing so much as to be rid

of Julian and give herself breathing-space before they
had to team up again in order to deliver the posters.

'You won't be able to get into the town hall car park
today without a pass. The mayor gave John and me one
each for our cars last night. It's the senior citizens' lunch
today, and they've reserved all the car park spaces for the
helpers who are ferrying in the old folk.'

And, being a Saturday, it would be impossible to find
another parking space anywhere in the town by now.
Julian had got it all mapped out before he'd taken her
home last night, and he had not said a word to her then.

Instead, he had allowed her to come to the hospital
this morning, believing she would be independent of
him and his transport. Playing with her, in fact, as a cat
plays with a mouse, Berry fumed.

She was caught in a cleft stick.

The mayor had promised to keep his office open for
half an hour at mid-morning to enable them to collect
the posters, and it was nearing that time now. Julian's
intervention had more than doubled the time she'd
expected to take in measuring up the new wing, and the
town hall was more than two miles away from the
hospital, much too far for her to get there on foot before
the office closed.

She could not go back on her promise to help the
mayor distribute the leaflets, since he had so generously
agreed to give his own time to help her with the far more
onerous task of becoming secretary to her campaign.

It was fast becoming Julian's campaign, and Berry's
anger knew no bounds as she waited by the doors of
casualty while Julian went to collect his car from its
parking slot.

An off-duty nurse came out while she stood there, and
Berry glanced at her, and away again. She avoided Tina

Brown whenever possible. The girl was small, quick and bird-like, and pecked up any crumbs of scandal that the hospital had to offer. It was meat and drink to her, and it was clear that she had already heard the latest.

'Going out with our new consultant, then, are we?' She sidled up to Berry.

'We're going to deliver posters, that's all.'

'D'you expect me to believe that? Doesn't let the grass grow under his feet, our Mr Vyse, does he? Fellas usually want thanking *after* they take you out, not before.'

Laughing at the success of her gibe, which drained the blood from Berry's cheeks, Tina Brown darted away as Julian drew the Jaguar to a halt and came round to open the passenger door for Berry. His keen look took in the figure of the retreating nurse and Berry's pale cheeks, but he made no comment except to say, 'Give me your bag. I'll put it in the boot. It'll save you from having to nurse it.'

Berry felt as if she would have liked its comforting familiarity in her lap, but she felt incapable of protest, and she hunched into her seat, trying to remove herself as far from Julian as the limited space allowed, as he steered the long car through the busy shopping streets towards the town hall.

Once there, Berry found herself drawn into the cheerful bustle of activity, and some of the sting from the nurse's malicious remarks receded a little.

The mayor's staff proved their efficiency by having the posters packed ready in shoulder-bags for easy carrying, and Julian grinned as Berry slid her bag over her shoulders.

'You make a cute little paper-boy.'

He had called her decorative the evening before. Berry

switched her mind away from the memory, and said
shortly, 'This bag's nearly down to my feet. I'll have to
shorten the strap, somehow, before we start out.'

She started to swing the bag from off her shoulders,
and Julian intervened. 'Leave it where it is. I'll adjust it
while it's on you, then you'll be sure it's riding at a
comfortable level.'

His suggestion made sense, but the behaviour of her
pulse when he touched her did not, and Berry felt the
reverse of comfortable as she waited impatiently for him
to pull the webbing strap through the wide buckle.

'Say when?'

'Now. It's fine just here,' Berry threw over her
shoulder disjointedly.

She held the bag at hip level, where she could reach its
contents easily, and wished Julian would hurry up and
fix the buckle and allow her to go free.

She felt like a puppy held on a leash, with his hands
holding on to the strap, and the second she felt it take the
weight of the bag again she erupted away from him and
said hurriedly, 'You take the shops on the other side of
the road. I'll take the ones on this side.' Ignoring the
mocking glint in his eyes that derided her panic she
dived into the refuge of the nearest one.

Word of what they were doing had gone ahead of
them, and soon a rash of posters began to appear in their
wake in shop windows on either side of the street, in
spaces made ready for their arrival.

Berry could see Julian popping in and out of the shops
on his side of the street, already well ahead of her, they
were like two figures on a weather house, she thought
without humour. Storm and sunshine, appearing and
disappearing; and she wondered who related to which.

Julian was waiting for her when she reached the end of

the street, and added to her disgruntled frame of mind
by chiding, 'Come on, slowcoach. We've got five more
streets to get through yet.'

By the end of the third, Berry was beginning to flag,
and felt tempted to make inroads into a large bar of
chocolate given to her by one of the shopkeepers as a
raffle prize.

She used it instead as a trophy to flaunt in front of
Julian, and was sorely put out when he raised his
eyebrows and said loftily, 'Is that all you've got? I've
had half a dozen donations from my side of the street.
Let's break for lunch before we do the other two streets,'
he added, and Berry said hastily,

'A sandwich will do for me. I've got to take a poster
into this take-away. I'll get one from here.'

Julian could go and get himself a meal in a restaurant
if he wanted to. She hoped he would, and she could do
her sides of the last two streets on her own, and hopefully
collect some donations too, to restore her deflated ego.

She turned away into the shop, pulling out a poster,
and to her chagrin Julian followed her, and she could not
retreat when a small boy caught sight of her and
shouted, 'Mum, shop!'

A motherly looking woman appeared, bearing a tray
of freshly made filled rolls, and her face broke into a wide
smile upon seeing Julian.

'Why, Mr Vyse, this is a surprise! What brings you
here again? Jamie's fine now. His limp's quite gone.'

'I'm the one who needs help this time,' Julian smiled.
'We're begging.' He nodded towards the poster in
Berry's hands, and the woman took it from her and
offered instantly,

'I'll put this in the window, and another one inside the
shop if you've got one to spare. We owe you a lot, David

and I, for all the hours you've spent here, teaching him to walk again.'

'You know the need of a children's ward better than most,' Julian acknowledged, 'although people have taken in the posters willingly enough. We're just going to have a break now, before we do our final two streets.'

'Have you eaten?'

'Not yet.'

'Then take these. I know you like cheese. And I'll think of some way to raise some money for your ward. No, put that back,' adamantly, as Julian fished out a handful of coins from his pocket, 'it's my turn to do something for you.'

Refusing payment, she waved away their thanks, and turned to serve a queue of other customers that was forming behind them.

'Are they private patients of yours?'

Berry was not interested, but anything was better than allowing the silence between them to stretch as she perched beside Julian on the harbour wall to eat their food.

Their legs dangled over the shingle, on which were drawn up a number of fishing-smacks, waiting to be floated off on the next tide, and Julian shared the rolls between them, and bit into his own appreciatively as he answered, 'No. What makes you think they might be?

'The boy's mother said you'd spent a lot of time there, teaching him to walk.'

'Only because he couldn't come to the hospital. He was too young at the time to come by himself, and his mother was just recently widowed, and struggling to get the take-away on its feet. It was a new venture, and it would have gone hard with her to have to lose half a day's takings to bring the lad into hospital for therapy, after he broke his hip. And I'd got nothing to tie me when I was off duty, so it was easier for me to come to treat him at home.'

For nothing, he meant, no one.

Berry had unaccountable difficulty in swallowing her mouthful of cheese roll, and turned her eyes on the fishing-smacks as a cheerful voice hailed them from one of the decks.

'Good day, Mr Vyse. When are you coming out with us again?'

'As soon as I can get a free minute,' Julian called back. 'I'll let you know.'

'Do you go out fishing with the smacks?' Berry regarded Julian with undisguised surprise. It was the antithesis of his normal occupation, and a vision of him clad in sou'wester and rubber boots did not accord with the elegant consultant she knew, but he seemed to be on easy terms with the fishermen, as he had been with the mother and child at the take-away.

He was a curious mixture, she reflected, as Julian replied, 'I go as often as I can. It's a different world out there. Just you against nature. I find it the perfect antidote to my own work, when I need one.'

He had needed an antidote badly when she had first seen him in the hospital chapel, and Berry wondered if he had gone down to the harbour that night, after he left her, and worked out his torment in the elemental world of the sea. But it was something she could not ask him without risking a snub, although Julian did not seem averse to asking personal questions himself. He asked one now.

'What do you do in your spare time?'

'I—er—oh, the hospital radio takes up most of it.'

She did not do much else these days, Berry realised

suddenly. Nearly all her social contacts came through her work at the hospital radio, and up to now she had been content for it to remain like that.

Socially, her life since she had come to Aldermouth had been spartan, deliberately so, since she had needed the breathing space to enable her to recover from Chris. But now she had got her life organised again there was no real need for her to continue to deprive herself.

Was that, perhaps, the reason for the unaccountable restlessness that had assailed her lately? From her present position of comparative emotional security, did she now feel the need for something new in her life to fill the gap Chris had left?

Without thinking, she turned and looked up at Julian, and her mind recoiled, and warned her, 'Some*thing*, not some*one*.'

Don't be silly! she scorned its flight of fancy as Julian asked her again, 'No dates? Not even on a Saturday night? Working for the new ward should soon alter that.'

'I've got a date in the studio at St Luke's at four o'clock this afternoon,' Berry answered abruptly. 'We start broadcasting early on a Saturday. If we don't get moving, we shan't get the last two streets done in time for me to get back.'

Julian had arbitrarily taken over this Saturday, but if he had got any designs on organising her future spare time, he could think again. She was quite capable of organising her own life, and the campaign for the new ward, without his help, and to demonstrate it she tossed the last of her cheese roll to a hopefully cruising gull and swung her feet back over the wall at a speed that put her in dire risk of landing on the shingle below.

Julian put out a swift hand to act as a safety net at her

back but, ignoring it, she swung her bag purposefully across her shoulder as her feet found terra firma on the harbour top, and set off at a brisk pace to complete her task.

The bag was a lot lighter now than when she'd started, and it was quite empty by the time the last two streets were finished. Julian took it from her and put it over his own shoulder, as they battled their way back through the shopping crowds to reach the town hall.

The civic clock pointed to nearly ten minutes to four, and Berry regarded it with dismay. 'We'll have to get a move on,' she urged Julian as he left the bags with the commisionaire, and let her into the Jaguar. 'I promised the children I'd read them a story, and they'll be waiting for it.'

'I'll get you there on time, don't worry.'

Get me to the church on time . . . The analogy struck a sour note, but Berry reluctantly had to admire the skill with which Julian wove the big car in and out of the rush-hour traffic, manoeuvring it with a confident dexterity, as if it were no bigger than a Mini.

It was still only a couple of minutes to four when he stopped at the porter's lodge and retrieved the studio key for her, and took Berry right up to the hospital entrance before reversing and running the Jaguar back to the car park proper.

With a hasty, 'Thanks for the lift,' Berry fled, grateful for the excuse to leave him behind, when otherwise good manners would have demanded that she walk with him at least as far as the lifts. And that she most definitely did not want to do.

In case Julian's longer legs might catch up with her, she ran up the stairs instead of waiting for the lift. And, if the start of her story was somewhat breathless, it was unlikely that the children would complain. When John put in an appearance half an hour later, to do his stint of announcing, the familiar routine had restored Berry to normal.

Saturday was always a busy night at the hospital, with new admissions and extra visiting time, and Berry always tried to have something specially interesting for those patients who had no visitors, and who might otherwise feel left out of things.

After the children's programme was over she launched into a brief résumé of what they had done so far towards getting the new ward, carefully leaving out mention of individual names. She was only too well aware that the hospital grapevine must be already making capital of the fact that she and Julian had been delivering posters together.

Now that that preliminary task was done, however, she would be able to avoid him, Berry assured herself, so the gossips would have nothing to feed on.

The operating theatre was back in running order again, so Julian should be returning to work during the mornings and, apart from an occasional meeting, when the whole of the committee would be present and act as a sponge to soak up some of his relentless drive, she need have no further contact with him.

Cheered by the thought, she left John playing a disc over the air in the usual late Saturday evening programme of dedications, and went in search of Trish and coffee. She felt she needed both tonight and, although Trish might tease, at least she would do it without malice.

Berry was humming the latest request tune out loud as she pushed open the door to the ward office. The kettle was ready plugged in, and the coffee-jar was on the desk, but the ward sister was missing.

Berry glanced along the ward in search of her, and from the end Trish raised her hand in a quick signal that mimed, 'Switch on. I won't be five minutes,' before she disappeared behind curtains drawn round a bed.

'Trouble?' Berry enquired as Trish joined her soon afterwards, and the ward sister answered,

'Nothing much. Just a concussion case wanting a bit of peace and quiet. He should be fine in a day or two.'

'There'll be big trouble if you don't make that three cups of coffee, instead of two,' a stern voice warned, and Berry swung round, with the boiling kettle dangling precariously from her suddenly nerveless fingers.

Julian took it from her and said to Trish, 'This woman is a walking potential accident. You really will have to get her better trained.'

'Why? What's Berry been up to that I don't know about?'

'She nearly took a header off the top of the electrician's steps when she was measuring up the playroom this morning. And then, afterwards, she almost fell off . . .'

He was going to say, fell off the patient-trolley. He was going to use the episode to torment her, knowing how raw she felt about it. Berry glared at the consultant. Her eyes hated him for what he was about to do to her. If he tried to make a fool of her in front of Trish, she would never forgive him.

Green eyes glinted down into her face, reading the storm of protest that darkened her mobile features, showing her feelings as clearly as if they were words printed on a page.

Steam rose between them from the kettle spout. It reminded Berry of a volcano about to erupt. Which was what Julian would discover she could do, if he so much as said a word. Just one. Berry's eyes blazed up into his.

'. . . she almost fell off the harbour wall, feeding her lunch to a seagull,' he said, and his eyes jeered at her suspense.

Berry sent him a look of pure fury. She was limp with relief yet tight with temper, and felt like a Yo-Yo between the two as Trish complained, 'The water in that kettle will be cold before it reaches the coffee if you don't pour it out soon.' And she spooned granules into three mugs to hasten her much-needed reviver.

Berry took her own mug and buried her face in its depths. The heat of it made her blink, and her hands shook as they cocooned the serviceable brown pottery. She felt so angry, she felt like hurling it, liquid and all, at Julian. And so relieved, that she felt a silly prick at the back of her eyes, and blinked again, blaming it on the steam.

Julian leaned casually on the end of the office desk, sipped, and said, 'This is nice, Trish. It's just like old times.'

'I'll leave you to talk them over together.' Berry seized her chance to get away.

'No, you won't. You'll sit still and finish your coffee, and don't be such a goose.' Trish stopped her. 'Julian and I used to work together, we didn't walk out together, so we haven't got any dark secrets to talk about.'

It was too late to wish that her meeting with Julian this morning in the new ward complex was a secret. It would be all over the hospital by now, with infinite variations and, if Trish hadn't already heard about it, it would not be long before she did.

Miserably, Berry took comfort in her coffee, and the ward sister had to repeat her remark twice before it dawned upon her that Trish was talking to her, and not to Julian.

'Wake up.' Trish jogged her back to life. 'You were miles away.'

'Sorry.' Berry heartily wished that were true. 'What were you saying?'

'Julian was saying that it would be nice if we got together again, now that he's settled in Aldermouth. So how about coming to my place one evening, for supper?'

'Count me out,' Berry refused promptly. 'I'll be decorating the playroom every spare minute I can get.'

The last thing she wanted was to partner Julian in a foursome, and probably fuel even more gossip, and she turned the consultant's own words back on him with the perfect excuse, 'If we're to get the playroom finished within the month, I shan't be able to drag my feet.'

She could feel Julian's green glance level at her over the rim of his coffee-mug, as he retorted, 'Why not wait until the playroom's finished, and then we can all have supper together, to celebrate the event?'

Neatly trumping Berry's carefully played ace!

# CHAPTER FIVE

BERRY was getting ready to go out the following morning when she heard a car stop in the street below. She peered curiously through the curtain, in time to see Julian get out of the Jaguar and walk round the car towards the boot.

What was he doing here?

Berry ducked hurriedly out of sight from the window and stood tensely in the middle of the room, her hairbrush forgotten in her hand, and her mind a riot of questions.

Had Trish changed her mind and decided to invite them to supper tonight, after all? But, surely, if she had, she would have telephoned direct? Unless, of course, she had suggested it to Julian during his ward round, and the consultant had offered to deliver the message on his way home.

If so, he had wasted his journey, Berry told herself with satisfaction. She had the perfect excuse to be able to refuse any invitation for this evening.

The crunch of sticking wood resisting a pushing hand warned her that she would learn the reason for Julian's visit soon enough and, for a brief moment of cowardice, she contemplated not answering the door. She had more reason than ever, now, not to want to be seen in Julian's company.

Reason soon denied her that escape route, however.

There was no other exit from the flat, except via the front door. Her journey this morning had a time limit and, if she was going to set out at all, it had to be soon.

If she did not answer the door, and Julian chose to sit in his parked car outside, assuming that she had attended early service, and might be coming back soon, she would be trapped.

Her pride would refuse to allow her then to go ignominiously downstairs and bump into him and admit that she had be skulking behind a closed door in order to avoid seeing him, making him believe that she was afraid.

Her door-knocker rattled a tattoo and, taking a deep breath, Berry put down her hairbrush and went to answer it.

Julian greeted her with, 'I've come to return your shoulder-bag. Can I come in?'

'I'm just going out myself.'

Mentally, Berry cursed the haste with which she had left him the previous afternoon. It would not have mattered all that much if the children's story had been a few minutes late in starting, but she had been in such a hurry to leave Julian behind that she had completely forgotten her bag was locked in the boot of his car.

Common courtesy demanded that she should not keep him standing outside the door and, reluctantly, she stood aside and opened it wide. He came in, put the bag down on the table, and enquired, 'Were you going to church?'

'Not this morning. I'm taking the microphone into the hospital chapel this evening, to broadcast the service from there.'

His eyebrows arched. 'Outside broadcasts? It sounds quite ambitious.'

'Not only outside broadcasts. We do live ones whenever possible. Taped ones when we can't.'

'Where this morning, then?'

It was none of his business where she was going to this morning, and Berry felt tempted to tell him so outright, but she could not very well be rude when he had taken the trouble to drive over to return her bag, so she modified her sharp retort to, 'If you must know, I'm going to the warehouse for the materials to decorate the children's wing. It opens on a Sunday morning, to allow traders to pick up their goods.'

'Is it necessary to use your precious Sunday morning to collect it? Surely one of the days in the week ...?'

'Now who's dragging their feet?' she jeered. 'It's absolutely necessary, or I wouldn't be doing it. My neighbour's in the trade, and he's arranged with the warehouse manager for me to pick up whatever I need, so long as I do it today. Besides, two of the junior technicians have volunteered to wash down the walls of the playroom tomorrow, so I need the emulsion to start painting the walls with on Tuesday.'

'Tuesday will suit me fine.'

'Suit *you*?' Berry cast him a look of wary premonition.

'Fine,' he repeated gravely. 'I'm off duty on Tuesday. Did you imagine I'd leave you to do the job on your own?'

Her wildest imaginings did not envisage the senior consultant at St Luke's being able to leave anyone to do anything without his close supervision. Nevertheless, it had simply not occurred to Berry that he might take a hand in the purely practical aspect of the work. She had looked forward to being left to tackle that part of the job, at least, on her own, and in peace.

Now, she knew resignedly that it had been wishful thinking on her part. Julian was the type who had to be in the thick of things, organising everybody else, even if he did not lift a paint-brush himself.

Berry hoped fervently that his presence would not put off the junior members of staff whom she had recruited as voluntary labour. The prospect of it made her feel like opting out herself, but first she had to deal with his unwelcome presence in her flat.

'Would you like a coffee?' she enquired politely, in a tone that hoped he would refuse.

'Not now, thanks. I've just had my breakfast.'

Berry's more friendly accents mirrored her relief. 'In that case, I'll be off. The warehouse only stays open for a couple of hours on a Sunday.'

'I assume they'll deliver the stuff you choose, direct to the hospital.'

'It's a cash and carry only. The stuff can be stored under lock and key in the new wing, and be ready for whenever we need to use it.'

'The boot of your vehicle's rather small, to take a load of that size.'

'I should be able to do it in two trips, so if I leave right away ...' Berry edged significantly towards the door.

'Where do you keep your car? I didn't see it in the street when I came in.'

'There's a row of garages at the back of the flats. I have to walk round the block to get there.'

She would have to run round the block if Julian did not go soon, she thought crossly, and gave her door keys a suggestive jingle.

'Save yourself the trouble. The boot of my car will practically cope with a house removal. We'll go in the Jaguar, and do the journey in one.'

It was so logical, so infuriatingly the sensible thing to do, and the last thing Berry wanted.

'You'll be needed at the hospital,' she hoped transparently, and stiffened at the look Julian slanted at her as he retorted,

'I've already done my ward rounds. And I don't operate on a Sunday unless it's an emergency.'

Julian himself constituted an emergency of the first water, Berry thought crossly, and one that, so far, she had been singularly unsuccessful in coping with.

If he tries to change the things I've ordered, I'll scream, she promised herself as, soon afterwards, he backed the Jaguar into a parking slot beside the gaunt warehouse building which was sited discreetly out of the town. They made their way through the turnstile, to where materials of every description were stacked in wholesale quantities.

Julian took charge of the trolley and gleefully Berry let him. If he insisted upon them collecting the whole order in one, he would find it as heavy to push as a tractor by the time they got round the warehouse!

With malicious satisfaction, she loaded the trolley with tins of paint, emulsion, ceiling white, wallpaper, and packs of nursery cut-outs, regretting that she had not offered to obtain the floor tiles for the contractor as well.

To her chagrin, Julian showed no sign of strain, and cruised the trolley alongside her with as much ease as if he were merely collecting a few days' groceries.

She noticed he inspected each item carefully as she placed it in the trolley. Checking to see if he could find fault with her choice, and alter something, Berry surmised with gritted teeth, but he made no comment until they reached the check-out point.

'I'll see to this,' he said, and reached towards his top jacket pocket.

'It's down to my neighbour's account.' Berry's voice

was dangerously quiet. 'This is a wholesale warehouse, for traders only. Ask the manager, if you don't believe me. If he did stretch a point and allow you to pay,' she raised her voice to cut off the beginnings of Julian's protest, 'if they did allow you to pay, they would charge the full retail price for every single item on the trolley.'

Her hard look challenged him to waste the fund's money in such an irresponsible manner, and Julian met it for a long, considering moment that made Berry's eyes begin to waver, so that she cut in quickly with,

'Let's get through the check-out before the crowd gets in front of us, or we'll be here all day.' She gestured towards a family bearing down on them with four trolley-loads of fancy goods, and threatening to usurp their place in the queue.

It made her feel good when the girl at the till took her neighbour's account number, smiled and said, 'All the best, Miss Baker. You're doing a marvellous job.'

Berry felt the sweet taste of success in her mouth as she walked back to the car beside Julian, without offering to help him push the piled-up trolley.

The capacious boot of the Jaguar swallowed everything they put inside it with plenty of room to spare, just as Julian had predicted it would. After relinquishing the now empty wheeled container to the car park trolley-catcher, they were soon heading away from the warehouse, back towards the hospital, with plenty of time to spare.

Julian broke the silence. 'As soon as we get rid of this lot, we'll ...' He broke off as a high-pitched buzzing sounded from the dashboard, and he reached forward questing fingers to snap down a switch and answer the summons briefly with, 'Vyse here.'

'A call for you, from men's surgery, Mr Vyse,' a

disembodied voice answered. 'A concussion case has developed breathing problems.'

'I'll be there in under ten minutes. In the meantime, tell them to ...'

Julian gave terse instructions that his listeners would understand, but which passed over Berry's head, and the Jaguar ceased its easy cruising speed and leapt forward like a throughbred rowelled with a spur.

'That's the trouble with being a surgeon,' he mourned. 'Your life can never be completely your own.'

The look he directed at Berry as he said it seemed to carry some obscure kind of warning, but Berry dismissed the thought as pure fancy. Whatever the warning might be, it was too obscure for her, and she answered unsympathetically, 'You chose the job, and everything has its drawbacks. You can't very well refuse to go.'

'If I wanted to refuse, I wouldn't be linked by car radio direct to the hospital. But it's a pity it had to happen today. I'd planned for us to drive out along the coast, and have lunch together at a little pub I know.'

He had *planned* ... He had not asked her if she would like to go, or even if she was free to do so. He had planned, and arrogantly assumed that she would fall in with his plans without question.

Berry's gorge rose. The man's arrogance fairly took her breath away, but she retained enough to thrust back, 'Your plans would have come unstuck anyway, so far as I'm concerned. I've got plans of my own.'

Her plans had included a grilled chop for lunch, washing her hair, and sticking her feet up with the latest bestseller until it was time to go back to the studio for the chapel broadcast, but Julian was not to know that. Before he could ask, they were running into the hospital car park, and Berry said quickly. 'Leave the boot open. I'll ask the porter to help me to take the materials into the new wing.'

'Hang about a bit, and I'll take you home. I may not have to be away for long.'

Interested eyes would see her waiting for Julian, and were no doubt watching them both together now, so Berry said quickly, 'I'll look after myself. You go ahead.' She added significantly, as Julian hesitated, 'I hope the trip hasn't delayed you for too long to save your patient.'

The reminder worked, as she had guessed it would. Without a word, Julian handed her the car keys and, pivoting on his heel, he hurried off in the direction of men's surgical.

Berry felt a prick of conscience as she fetched the spare patient-trolley from the new wing and began to load it with the contents of the car boot.

It was a rotten thing to do, to use a patient's difficulties to solve her own, and she kept her fingers superstitiously crossed for the young man with concussion, as she transferred her morning's purchases to their new home.

Afterwards, she locked the car boot, and left the keys in the porter's lodge for Julian to collect when he came out again, then considered her own position without transport. If he had not interfered with her arrangements in the first place, she would have made the double journey easily from the warehouse, and still have been left with the use of her own car afterwards.

Now, she was stranded.

Buses in Aldermouth were few and far between on a Sunday. The main tourist season was over, and the sightseeing runabouts were off the roads until next year. Glancing at her watch, Berry saw that she had precious little prospect of getting back to her flat before it was almost time to turn round and come right back again.

When Julian returned, she intended to be long gone. She was not sure where to, but anywhere would do, so long as it was far enough away from the hospital to avoid bumping into the senior consultant, leaving him to assume that she was going about the rest of her Sunday as she had originally planned—without him.

Her absence would teach him a much-needed lesson: that working together for the new children's ward did not give him prior right over her time.

Three hours was a long time to while away, however, before she was due in the studio. Berry ate an unsatisfactory snack of beans on toast in a small coffee-shop, where she thought Julian would be unlikely to seek her out if he became unexpectedly free.

Afterwards, she took herself off along the cliffs for a walk, but a soaking drizzle came in with the tide and drove her back again, and she was fast running out of her capacity to consume any more coffee by the time the hands of her wristwatch released her to return to St Luke's.

'Julian's been in here, looking for you,' John greeted her when she reached the studio, and Berry stiffened, then relaxed again as she remembered that the Jaguar had been gone from its parking slot when she'd come back to the hospital.

John went on, 'He said you might need a lift back home, but I told him I didn't know where you were going this afternoon. Or who with,' he added wickedly.

Berry suppressed a grin. So far, so good! John had proved an unwitting accomplice, and Julian could draw whatever conclusion he liked from her absence.

The two volunteers came on duty to enable herself

and John to go to the chapel early to fix up the necessary broadcasting equipment, and Berry cast a wary glance round her as she helped to carry the paraphernalia across to the chapel, but there was still no sign of the Jaguar, and for the next hour or two she was too busy to give Julian's whereabouts much thought.

A similiar broadcast of the harvest festival services had proved to be so popular with the patients that tonight the vicar was putting on a hymn-singing service. Once it had started, requests and dedications followed one another in a rousing chorus, in which Berry joined enthusiastically, until her voice felt hoarse with the combination of announcing and singing, and she was glad to relinquish the microphone to the vicar for the final blessing.

After that, John took over, closing the programme to the wards, and handing them back to the studio for the next half-hour of listeners' letters, and the congregation broke up and made for the door.

Berry had her arms full of wires and gadgets when Julian's voice spoke from behind her, and nearly caused her to drop them again.

'When you're ready to go, I'll take you home.'

'I'm not. I mean . . . I don't want . . . I'll be ages yet. John will give me a lift back when we've both finished.'

She had done everything she could to avoid giving Julian his own way, and taking her back home again. And now, just when she thought she had succeeded, he had turned up again, like the proverbial bad penny.

When she'd seen his parking space was empty, Berry had thought herself to be safe, and she could have groaned out loud in frustration at his unexpected reappearance.

'You get off home, Berry.' John came up, similarly

burdened, and overheard her. 'A couple of the choirboys
have stayed behind to help carry all the equipment back
to the studio. You've earned yourself an evening off for
once, lugging all that paint and stuff from the warehouse
this morning.'

'Indeed she has,' the vicar agreed amiably. 'I'll walk
to the car with you. I'm going on to the wards myself,
now.'

There was no help for it. Berry relinquished her
armful of equipment to a fresh-faced teenager, and
turned reluctantly to walk between the two men,
fulminating at the fate that had conspired against her.

Julian chose his arena each time with an unerring
touch, she thought bitterly. The chapel was no place in
which to engage in verbal fisticuffs and, with the cleric
stopping to chat as they reached the Jaguar, there was no
way she could lie herself out of accepting a lift.

Trish was off duty that evening, so she had not even a
promised cup of coffee as an excuse.

With an ill grace, she dropped into the now familiar
car seat, and leaned her head back against the rest,
making weariness that was not altogether feigned her
excuse not to talk.

Julian, too, seemed to be immersed in his own
thoughts as the big car ran silently through the Sabbath
quiet of the evening streets. Perhaps his mind centred on
his patient? Berry found herself wondering if the
consultant, too, felt weary.

He worked long hours, with a single-mindedness and
dedication that seemed to be the hallmark of everything
he did, including the campaign for the new ward.

If he felt tired tonight, it did not seem to affect the
unique magnetism that flowed from him as strongly as

ever, like an electric current, piercing the darkness of the car.

Tiredness made her extra vulnerable to its insidious probing, and Berry's nerves felt fiddlestring-taut when Julian stopped the car outside her flat, and turned in his seat to regard her with that same single-minded concentration that made her spine feel suddenly weak. Unnerved by his silent scrutiny, she blurted out the first words that came into her head.

'H-how was your patient?'

Surreptitiously, she searched with fumbling fingers to release her seat-belt lock, and encountered a set of long, strong fingers, bent on the same errand. She tried to snatch her hand away, but the fingers sprang the lock with quick efficiency, and enclosed her own in the same swift, decisive movement.

Berry caught a sharp breath as she found her hand trapped, and Julian answered, 'He's feeling a bit sorry for himself, but he should be all right now. Thank you for asking, just the same. You've got a kind heart, Rowanberry.'

That was what John called her, when he was in a teasing mood.

On Julian's lips, it had an entirely different ring, and Berry's heart began a slow, hard thudding inside her breast. Her caught breath had to last her, because Julian's lips came down and covered her mouth before she had time to take another.

His kiss grew deeper, searching, bringing back the starburst to her veins. His roving lips spoke a silent language of their own, and her mouth pursed under the pressure, striving to answer.

Was this the way he had kissed his wife?

Perhaps even as Julian was kissing her, Berry, he was

making believe to himself that he was kissing Kathleen. Trying to stem his alone-ness with self-delusion, regardless of the effect his kiss was having upon her.

Such a thing was not unknown, and alarm bells rang in Berry's mind like a bugle call to arms. Kathleen's arms. With an inarticulate cry, Berry wrenched herself free, pushed open the car door, and catapulted on to the pavement, running up the area steps and into the lobby.

She rammed her key into the door lock and twisted it open, praying that the wood would not stick against her hand tonight. She gave a hunted look over her shoulder, but Julian had not moved from his seat in the car.

He was bending down slightly, to enable him to look after her through the still-open passenger door, watching her flight, and his voice floated after her mockingly.

'See you . . .'

He reached out and pulled the car door shut on his words, and the thud echoed the crunch of the house door as Berry gave it a mighty push. It let her through, and she ran up the stairs, to the blessed sanctuary of her flat.

The rear lights of the Jaguar winked at her derisively as she watched from the safety of the partially drawn curtains, while the red discs turned out of the close and disappeared. The erratic beat of her pulse began to steady a little, only to accelerate again as she turned back into the room, and confronted her shoulder-bag, still sitting on the table where Julian's hand had placed it that morning.

Furious with herself for reacting to his kiss, Berry bundled the bag out of sight in a cupboard, and slammed the door on it.

But she could not slam the door on her own thoughts.

Julian was a disturbingly attractive man and, no matter how much she disliked him and resented his unwelcome interference in her life, each time he touched her, her own inherent femininity responded to that attraction in a manner that was a warning in itself.

Not that she needed any warning, she assured herself. She was not a junior nurse, to be dazzled by the handsome senior consultant. Chris had long since extinguished any stars from her eyes, and these days her gaze was very clear-sighted, and not a little cynical when it rested upon men.

Any attraction she might feel towards Julian was purely physical, and she would make sure it was kept well under control. *Her* control, not his.

Berry saw nothing of Julian when she went to the studio the next day. She was later than usual, and found John immersed in a small mountain of paperwork.

'Bail me out, do,' he begged distractedly. 'I'm trying to co-ordinate so many coffee mornings, jumble sales, whist drives, nearly-news—what on earth's a nearly-new?—and now the ward staff want to hold an auction, of all things.'

'Good for them,' Berry enthused, and reached into the table drawer. 'Take over the mike for a few minutes, and give those letters to me. I've started a calendar, to make sure the functions don't clash with one another.' She ran a finger down the days. 'What about the Saturday morning after next? There's nothing else on that day, and it'll give the staff time to collect things together. They could hold the auction in the car park if it's fine, or in the new children's ward if it's wet.'

She slotted the various events into the calendar, and rang the mayor's wife with the details, to make sure they got all possible publicity. Then taking the microphone back from John, she swung into the routine of children's story, bingo numbers, request records, leaving the final

news items to John, including the latest total of
donations to the fund.

It would cause Trish to raise her eyebrows when she
came back on duty tomorrow night, Berry thought, but
her pleasure in the prospect of imparting the news was
marred by the possibility that Julian might make a habit
of partaking of coffee in the ward sister's office, if he
happened to come in during the evening to check on a
patient.

She was not well acquainted with Trish's deputy, so
she happily gave the ward office a miss. But, when she
got outside, Julian's car was not in the car park, and she
had deprived herself of much needed refreshment for
nothing.

Perhaps the concussion case was on the mend, and the
consultant had reverted to his usual routine of coming to
St Luke's during the mornings only?

'If he has, it will let me out,' Berry told herself
thankfully, and then remembered that tomorrow was
Tuesday, Julian's day off, and he intended to spend it
helping to decorate the playroom.

The two technicians had made excellent progress,
Berry saw when she reached the playroom on the
following day. Not only had they scrubbed the walls and
the ceiling, but they had rubbed the paintwork down to
the wood as well, ready to take the first undercoat.

A couple of off-duty nurses were already busy with
emulsion and brushes, helped by one of the junior
doctors, and the houseman, who did not allow the
presence of his companions to inhibit his open delight
when Berry put in an appearance.

'You three carry on,' he told them, and basely
deserted them in favour of Berry. 'I'll help you, if you'll
tell me what you're going to do,' he offered with a wide

grin that reminded Berry of the Cheshire cat.

She felt a flash of irritation at his obviousness. Life at the moment was complicated enough, without the houseman making it worse.

'Don't break off what you're doing. I'll help Berry,' Julian said, and strolled through the door to join them.

The houseman regarded the arrival of his senior with frank dismay. 'Oh—er—good afternoon, sir. I didn't know you were coming along as well.'

Clearly, he had expected to have the field to himself, but to his credit he stuck to his guns. 'I'm sure anything I can do to help Miss Baker——' he persisted.

Berry intervened hastily, 'You can help on Saturday week, if you're off duty. Come along to the auction. We need as many people as we can get, as well as all the goods you can spare.'

'What sort of goods?' The houseman looked ready to bring his all, and Berry suppressed a desire to laugh.

'Anything in good condition will do. I'm bringing along a table lamp, which should sell for a pound or two,' she steered him tactfully.

She felt she needed someone to steer *her*, as the afternoon dragged on.

Each time she turned, she found Julian and the houseman at her elbow. When she separated nursery cut-outs from their backing, each of them was there, wanting to hold a corner. When it came to putting the cut-outs on the walls, Julian effectively got rid of the houseman for a while by directing him up the ladder to do the job, immediately drew Berry to another part of the room, and made use of her temporarily redundant hands by demanding her help with something else, which he could quite easily have done by himself.

As soon as the houseman was finished with the cut-outs, he was back, clearly disgruntled by his senior's treatment, and Berry's patience snapped.

The silent duelling was getting on her nerves. She felt like a bone being snarled over by two contesting terriers, and knew uneasily that the contest was being closely watched by the other volunteers in the room, and would be avidly discussed as soon as her back was turned.

Julian was just doing it to be awkward, she fumed. He could not resist showing his authority, and today it was the unfortunate houseman who was catching the brunt of it, instead of herself.

He was callously using her as a whip with which to belabour his junior, and Berry hated him for doing it.

At length, in exasperation, she declared, 'I've had enough for today. I'm going home,' and rounded angrily on Julian as he turned to accompany her to the door. 'I don't need a lift. I've got my own car.'

She marched away, leaving the houseman openly disconsolate, and Julian's narrowed eyes following her, piercing her back as far as the door and beyond it, so that, even after she had slammed it behind her, she had to consciously stop herself from breaking into a run across the car park.

By the end of the following week, the playroom was finished. In the interim, Berry had used all her cunning to avoid both Julian and the houseman, and had largely succeeded, owing to them both being occupied with a visiting medical team from abroad.

The contractor laid the floor, and Berry attended to the final touches, her own *pièce de résistance* automatic window blinds that could be folded two ways, to give a different nursery-rhyme scene on each.

She felt proud of the blinds. She had come across them quite by chance, and snapped them up triumphantly.

She felt proud of the fact that the room was completed before the month which Julian had stipulated.

Prouder still of the neat way she circumvented his plan to make the celebration supper a foursome only, with Trish and her husband.

'Let's turn it into an American supper,' she suggested slyly to the ward sister, adding for good measure, 'Julian suggested that we use it to celebrate finishing the playroom, so we can't very well leave out all the others. They've all helped with the decorating.'

'The others' amounted to about thirty people in all, who had come in spare minutes and between shifts, and Berry felt well pleased with her strategy when they all foregathered in the newly decorated room for the supper on the last evening.

In such a sizeable gathering, Julian would be just one of the crowd, and she should be able to dodge him quite easily. All the committee were present, and the mayor and his lady put on their chains of office in deference to the presence of the local press.

'The reporters have been good about giving us coverage in the newspapers,' John pointed out. 'It's our turn to help them, now. And, besides, the warehouse has sent a whole batch of brand-new toys. A public mention will be a good advert for their business, and a way of showing our thanks.'

The small room took on a festive air, with the gift toys and child-sized furniture ranged round the walls, and the buffet table at the top, giving room for the guests to mill around and chat in the centre.

Berry and Trish had both been busy baking, and two of the canteen ladies took charge of the tea and coffee urns. The houseman produced bottles of table wine as his contribution, and basked in Berry's delighted thanks until Julian appeared, and sent the sun in for his junior by placing his offering of bottles of champagne beside them.

'Did you *have* to outclass him so obviously?' Berry hissed furiously, conscious of the houseman's downcast face. She could cheerfully have slain Julian, and the urge to do so did not diminish when he remarked blandly,

'You'll need something to drink to the success of the campaign. We're only half-way through it yet.'

'We finished the playroom in well under the month you wanted.'

'Time to congratulate ourselves when the whole lot is done. In the meantime, a drop of champagne might encourage the helpers to redouble their efforts.'

'The houseman's dinner wine would have done just as well. This isn't a civic function.'

'The ironmongery Prentiss and his wife are wearing say it is.'

Julian smiled in a cordial manner to the two dignitaries, and Berry had to do the same, hoping that her set grin did not look as forced as it felt.

She had to hope even harder shorly afterwards, when Julian compounded his sins by putting his arm round Berry's shoulders, and drawing her close to him when the newsmen called for, 'Photographs of the committee please, ladies and gentlemen.'

'You're not on the committee,' she reminded him in a furious undertone. 'I should have been photographed with John.'

'You've already been photographed with John.'

So she had, along with all the other committee members, but Berry knew with helpless rage that Julian's smiling description of herself as, 'Our charming chairperson,' and her photograph alongside the well known surgeon, would offer more front-page attraction to the media than any amount of school-type pictures of the whole committee bunched together.

Whether the press used it or not, Julian's action would be manna to the hospital gossips, and Berry seethed impotently that he should give even more impetus to the already busily wagging tongues.

She should be impervious to them by now, she knew, but undereneath her hard-won armour there still existed a sore patch that made her squirm at the knowledge that her name was once more being bandied about, and worse, coupled with that of Julian.

What further offences her *bête noire* might perpetrate during the evening Berry could only guess at, but fate in the guise of Julian's pocket buzzer intervened.

It came to life, and instantly the consultant broke off his conversation with the mayoress and reached for the day-room telephone. Berry surreptitiously crossed her fingers, and silently thanked her guardian angel when she heard him say. 'I'll come right away,' and instantly regretted allowing that seraph off duty when the consultant turned to the houseman and added, 'One of your patients, I believe. You'd better come along with me.'

It was just too slick to be true.

Taken at face value, Julian's action was that of a dedicated professional, inviting another professional along with him to see a case in whom they were both interested.

But Berry knew, she just *knew* that it was Julian wielding his authority yet again, making sure that, because he himself had to leave the party, the houseman was not allowed to remain either.

Her worst fears about the press photographers were

justified the next morning, and served to add to her mounting frustration. The reporters had latched on to Julian's description of her, as she had known they would, and she ground her teeth as she read the headlines above the picture of the two of them together.

'Our charming chairperson . . .'

With a muttered exclamation, Berry balled the innocent local daily in a fierce fist, and flung it into the waste-paper basket. Even a letter from the mayor, delivered by hand to the studio to congratulate her on the success of her efforts so far, did little to soothe her ruffled feelings. And things were made worse by a greeting from a batch of cheeky student doctors, as she made her accustomed round of the wards to get requests for the following day's programme.

'How's our charming chairperson today?' they chorused. 'Where's your other half?'

It took all her will-power to suppress her fury as she made careful notes of the requests with fingers that shook. She would make Julian pay dearly for his arrogance, if he continued to goad her, she vowed. In the event, it transpired that Julian paid in hard cash, although Berry paid the real, humiliating price.

John conducted the auction the following week. The day was sunny and mild, so they were able to spread themselves on the car park, and attracted a far larger crowd than they could have hoped to do indoors.

John had organised the props in style, with loud-speakers ranged round the car park so that no one should have the excuse of not being able to hear, and his cheerful patter soon had his would-be customers in a good humour.

Berry stood on the platform at his side, holding up the more portable items for easy viewing by those at the back of the crowd, and they quickly began to do a brisk trade.

An immense range of goods was on display. Berry's own table lamp was one of the first things to go. To her consternation, the houseman had contributed what looked like an almost new lawn-mower, and she thought she recognised a cherry-wood stool as being one she had seen in Julian's house.

He must want the ward very badly, if the stool had belonged to Kathleen, thought Berry.

An hour later, John's voice was rapidly becoming hoarse, and they had only one small item left to sell. He quickly knocked it down to an eager bidder, and mourned in an aside to Berry, 'We could have got rid of twice the amount. We'll have to organise another auction later on.' He turned back to face the crowd, and raised his voice once more.

'That's the lot for today, folks. A million thanks for your support. I only wish we had lots more to auction.'

'Why not auction a day out with Miss Baker?' an irrepressible junior doctor shouted back breezily. 'Come on, Berry, be a sport,' he begged. 'It's the chance we've all been waiting for.'

Taken aback, Berry turned to John for help. The student doctors were a harmless bunch, penurious and very hard-working but full of fun. Berry knew and liked them from occasional contacts in the hospital canteen but, true to her policy nowadays, she had always kept herself aloof from their overtures towards any closer friendship.

Patently, they regarded the auction as a golden opportunity to break through her barriers, and even John seemed to have no qualms about the outrageous suggestion, because he laughed and urged, 'Go on, Berry. Make him pay for the privilege. It's all in a good cause,' he persisted, noticing her hesitation.

It was a good cause, which she herself had promoted, and she could not be seen to back out when it came to making her own contribution. Masking her reluctance as best she could, Berry said doubtfully, 'If I really must.'

'Of course you must! It's a great idea. Who'll start the bidding?'

Amid a lot of banter, he suggested a price, and Berry became the focus of all eyes as the bids came in fast and furious from the crowd of young medics.

The houseman brought their antics to an abrupt halt by calling, 'A hundred pounds,' extracting a gasp from the onlookers, and far outbidding anything the students could afford.

John exulted, 'You've fetched more money than any of the other lots, Berry.'

He raised his hammer. 'Going, going . . .'

'Make that five hundred,' Julian's voice commanded.

# CHAPTER SIX

'IT isn't necessary to sell your favours for the sake of charity!' Julian's face was black with anger as he stormed into the studio in Berry's wake, like the wrath to come.

She spun to face him. 'It wasn't my idea, to auction myself.'

'You didn't seem averse to joining in the fun.'

'It was fun, until you interfered. And what do you mean by *favours*?'

Her life *had* been becoming fun again until Julian had appeared on the scene, and Berry hated him for spoiling her hard-won peace.

'You're the best one to know what you mean by favours, depending on how far you're prepared to go.'

'How dare you!'

The crack of Berry's hand across Julian's cheek rivalled the bang of John's gavel earlier, when he brought it down on the consultant's bid in a triumphant, 'Gone!'

Berry felt as if the sound would ring in her ears for the rest of her life.

The crowd had dispersed, and taken with them the news of the extravagant bid that would set the town alight. She hated Julian, and the crowd, and herself, for becoming the focus of even wider public attention.

She felt belittled and humiliated, and angrier than she had ever been in her life before, angrier than she had been with Chris. And, to add fuel to the furnace raging inside her, Julian dared to accuse her of selling her favours!

'I'll make you pay for that,' he gritted.

His face went chalk-white under its tan, except for a livid red weal across his cheek, where Berry's fingers had left their mark.

He grabbed them in a bone-crushing grip, jerking her to face him, and bruising lips vented his anger on her shrinking mouth.

Desperately, Berry fought him. She tried to raise her other hand, to imprint a matching angry pattern on his opposite cheek, but his long surgeon's fingers clamped her arm in bands of steel, holding her still.

His eyes were green fire, boring down into her upturned face. They wavered, and turned into jade pools, drowning her as his savage kiss cut off her breath, and Berry felt her senses begin to slip. With a tiny moan, she began to go limp in his arms.

His lips released her then, but his arms stayed tight round her as her heaving breast drew sufficient air for her to whisper thinly, 'I hate you for this.'

'Why just me? Why not all the others?' he snarled. 'Half the male staff in the hospital were bidding for you.'

'Not crazy, senseless bids like yours. Your five hundred pounds will set every tongue in the town wagging. Haven't you done enough damage in that direction already?'

'It's a bit late for you to worry about gossip. You didn't seem to mind the idea when you set yourself up for auction, so why the sudden hang-up now? Unless you've got a good reason?'

'What if I have? It isn't any business of yours. As it happens, my reason's simple enough. I've got a skin, not a hide.'

'So, you'll have to grow an extra layer to cover up.'

'There's an easier way. We'll cancel the whole thing. Withdraw your offer.'

'Never! I bid for you fair and square, and I'll hold you to the day out I'm paying for.'

'Yours wasn't a bid. It was sheer horse-trading.'

'So, I've got myself a nice little filly for the day.'

'Fillies can kick.'

Berry lashed out with both feet. In an excess of fury, she kicked as hard as her strength allowed. The soft soles of her slip-ons were incapable of inflicting real hurt, but the message they delivered was the same as if they had been clogs.

With a muttered exclamation, Julian sidestepped quickly out of range, and gritted, 'You've asked for this.' Shifting his hold on Berry, he upended her over his bent knee, and raised an angry palm.

John's voice saved her.

'Open the door, Berry, there's a love,' her producer shouted from the outside. 'My hands are full of tackle.'

Berry's feet found the floor, and she wriggled free just as Julian's hand was about to descend. She ran to the door and grabbed the handle, wrenching it open to reveal John, burdened with loudspeakers and wires.

'What's up with you two?' he wanted to know, his gaze ranging from one set face to the other as he dumped the tangle on to the table-top.

'Nothing,' Berry babbled. 'I'm late on the wards, that's all.'

She fled, with Julian's grim promise pursuing her, 'I'll call and pick you up tomorrow morning.'

Julian could call for her if he wanted to, but that was as far as he would get, Berry vowed. He could not force her to go out with him.

The knowledge did little to help her get to sleep. The clock struck the hours with remorseless regularity, and still she lay, tossing and wakeful, too tense to rest.

Julian had not said at what time he intended to come for her in the morning. For the umpteenth time, Berry turned gritty eyes on the illuminated dial of her alarm clock. If he came at nine o'clock, that was a mere seven hours from now.

Six hours. Five. Four.

Light filtered through the curtains before Berry finally dozed off, and she awoke with a start to find the sun shining, and the hands of the clock already leaving eight behind.

Time was of no account, since she did not intend to go out with Julian anyway. If he refused to call off the arrangement, she would, but she would be in a better position to tell him so if she was up, and properly dressed.

Her casual slacks and sweater were a silent statement of her intention, if Julian needed one, and Berry ate her sketchy breakfast with one eye on her bowl of muesli and the other constantly roving towards the window, in order to catch the first glimpse of the Jaguar as it came into the close.

When it came, she did not see it, after all. She was in the kitchen, putting her empty cereal bowl into the sink, and her first intimation that Julian was at the door was a loud rat-tat on the knocker.

Even the front door had let her down this morning. In deference to the continued fine weather, her below-stairs neighbour had propped it open and put her normal warning system out of action.

The cereal bowl clattered on to stainless steel from

Berry's suddenly nerveless fingers, and she froze against the work-top.

'Berry?' Julian's voice, stern and determined, penetrated the short hall. 'I know you're in there. I can hear you.'

Berry directed a vitriolic look at the hapless cereal bowl as Julian threatened,

'Open the door, or I'll crash it open.'

He was quite capable of carrying out his threat, and the possibility galvanised Berry into speech.

'Go away!' she called. 'I'm not coming out with you.'

'You're coming, if I have to drag you. You made the bargain, and you'll stick to it.'

'And give the gossips another field day? No, thanks.'

'You can either be the talk of the town, or the laughing stock of the town. Suit yourself. I've got a reporter from the *Crier* sitting in the car, and if you back out of the arrangement I'll see that he makes it front-page headlines. It'll look good, won't it? Our charming chairperson refuses to contribute to her own fund ...'

'You've got *what* in the car?'

The last part of his sentence passed Berry by. She flung open the door, and confronted Julian with an incredulous stare.

'Not what. *Who*. I've invited the man along to get news coverage of our day out. It'll make wonderful publicity for the ward fund.'

It would also stem any more gossip at source!

With unerring instinct, Julian had done the one thing calculated to turn what had become a joke in very bad taste into an act beyond criticism.

Why? Was he afraid of his own professional reputation? If he was, it was alien to his character as Berry knew him. She said faintly, 'I'll go and get changed.'

'Come as you are. You're just right. Bring an anorak
and a scarf, in case it gets windy.'

For the first time, it dawned upon Berry that Julian
was dressed as casually as she was herself, and with a
sense of unreality she reached into the hall cupboard and
hooked out an anorak and a bright scarf.

'Where . . .?'

'I'll explain when we get to the car. We haven't got
much time.'

The reporter increased Berry's bewilderment as
Julian set the Jaguar rolling, and the man greeted her
from the back seat with a cordial, 'I must say, Miss
Baker, it's pretty generous of you to give up your day out
to do this. You're a dedicated bunch of folk on the
hospital radio, aren't you?'

'This?' Berry turned suspicious eyes on Julian. What
had he let her in for now?

'You must come and listen to their broadcasts some
time,' Julian invited, saving her from having to reply.
'They do quite a lot of outside broadcasts. Some live.
Some taped, like this one today.'

He slanted a quick sideways look at Berry that
demanded she play along with him. She had no option,
Berry thought bemusedly. She felt too surprised to
speak.

Julian spoke directly to her. 'John put the recording
gear in the car boot, but you'll have to check it over
yourself before we get on the boat, to make sure that
nothing's missing. It all looks just a mess of wires to me.'

Recording equipment? Boat? What on earth was he
talking about?

Obliquely, Julian told her in his next remark to the
reporter. 'It was more than kind of the fishing skipper to
offer to turn out his smack on a Sunday, especially for us.

He gave the first donation to the fund. He was a patient of mine in St Luke's when the campaign was first launched, so he knows the value of the hospital radio from personal experience.'

'This sort of broadcast should go down well with the children.' The reporter was scribbling busily.

'It will,' Julian agreed. 'The skipper's offered to sponsor a crayoning competition for all the children who are patients at the hospital. The one who sends in the best picture of his or her idea of a fishing trip on his smack will get a free ride on his boat when they're better, and a fish dinner to take home afterwards. I fancy he'll choose a lot of winners, not just one. He's a kindly man, and a grandfather himself.'

Berry checked the recording equipment with her mind in a daze. Everything she needed was there, and the skipper's son carried it on board for her, while his father explained Julian's earlier haste when he said, 'You're just right for the tide. Another ten minutes, and it would have been on the turn.'

Pandering to his newly healed leg, the older man took the wheel, and they chugged out of the harbour, while his son did the heavier work of handling the fishing gear.

Julian helped Berry to set up her recording equipment where the chug of the diesel engine would not drown out other activity sounds, then he leaned with his back against the side of the boat, and his arms spread out on either side of him, and regarded her quizzically as she bent over the recorder.

'If you can't ad lib at such short notice, I'll help you.'

'I don't need your help. I've done as many off-the-cuff recordings as I've had hot dinners.'

If he expected her to be grateful to him for pitchforking her into this one, he had got another think coming! His outrageous bid for her time had started it all, and she would not lightly forgive him for that.

If it had been anyone but Julian, Berry would have accepted the offer of help gratefully enough, since she was ignorant of fishing-boat jargon. To Julian, it would all be familiar language, but she would make every mistake in the book rather than lower herself to ask him to interpret for her.

He had infiltrated into almost every aspect of her life, and she was determined to keep him out of the actual broadcast at all costs. Pretending to turn her back on the wind, Berry turned it on Julian as well, trying to shut out his presence. She might as well try to stop the wind from blowing!

She was edgily conscious of him close behind her, watching her every movement. She hunched her shoulders irritably against his invasive stare, but it refused to go away. When she switched on the recorder ready to announce the programme, tension sent her mind completely blank.

For the first time since she had started to broadcast, Berry dried up. Seconds stretched into minutes, and her tongue seemed to be stuck to the roof of her mouth.

Into a mind completely devoid of ideas, Julian's voice intruded. 'Having trouble?'

She could feel his eyes piercing her brain, reading the desert of emptiness that should be aflower with speech. Desperately, she unstuck her tongue, and answered jerkily, 'No—no trouble. The machine has to warm up first, that's all.'

Julian had confessed himself unfamiliar with the technicalities of recording, so hopefully he would not recognise her excuse as a lie. The machine would soon be red-hot if she did not do something quickly, she thought, panic-stricken. She could feel herself going hot and cold, and the palms of her hands were sticky with perspiration.

She would have to switch off, and pretend the machine was not working properly, and hope the reporter from the *Crier* was not one of those DIY enthusiasts who would offer to check it for her and find that nothing was wrong.

Berry reached out a trembling hand for the switch when the young fisherman called out, 'The net's going overboard now, Miss Baker. Do you see the marker buoy? We'll circle the boat in a wide arc, paying out the net as we go, until we come back to the buoy again, and then we haul it in.'

Bless the young fisherman for being both articulate and forthcoming! His cheerful shout shocked Berry's mind out of its paralysis and freed her speech. She drew in a deep shuddery breath and ad libbed swiftly, 'Hello, children. That was David, speaking from the *Harbour Belle*. David and his father are taking us out to catch some fish for the market.'

After that, experience took over. By means of adroit questioning, Berry led the young fisherman to explain the various stages of netting his catch, without once having to refer to Julian for guidance.

For a brief, exciting moment, she almost managed to forget the consultant as they reached the buoy and winched the bulging net inboard. Berry tried to avoid looking when the men began cleaning their catch, and instead concentrated her attention on the screaming cloud of gulls that followed the boat and made wild music into her microphone.

On the way back, the fisherman obligingly collected some earlier sown lobster-pots and Berry got roundly teased for backing away from the waving claws of the occupants.

'They're like huge spiders. Sea spiders,' she excused her shuddering cowardice. Then they were heading steadily back towards the harbour, and David took over the wheel while Berry taped the elderly skipper announcing details of his crayoning competition.

She finished off the broadcast herself with her usual formulae, and pocketed the tape with considerable satisfaction as the fishing-smack approached the harbour wall.

It was one of the best recordings she had done yet, but she remained tight-lipped, unwilling to give Julian the slightest credit and further boost his already inflated ego.

He vaulted up on to the hard as the diesel engine cut, and they glided in against the wall. With a practised hand, he caught the rope which the skipper flung to him, and tethered the fishing-smack to a nearby bollard. The reporter handed up the recording equipment to him, and turned to Berry.

'Your turn now, Miss Baker. Up you go.'

It was easier to board the smack than it was to disembark, Berry discovered. The side of the boat was a good foot below the stone walkway, and the deck lower still, and her short legs had not got enough stride to span one gap, let alone two.

The bobbing of the boat made matters worse, shortening and lengthening the gap with a disconcerting lack of regularity. Seeing her hesitate, Julian hunkered down on the wall-top and reached down both his hands towards her.

'Grab hold. I'll haul you up.'

'I'll get myself up. I'm not a sack of coal.'

'Don't be silly.' His voice was sharp. 'If you slip, you'll be crushed between the fishing-smack and the wall. The *Belle* isn't a light-weight rowing-boat.'

Julain seemed to be trying to crush her with his domineering ways, and Berry rebelled at being ordered about by him in front of the others.

'I'll manage. I'll stand on this box, and jump from there.'

She reached the top of the fish box, and might have retained her balance, but for a passing yachtsman who skimmed by and left a sizeable wash behind him, which sent the fishing-boat into a frenzied dance on the water.

Taken unawares, Berry staggered, and her arms described a wild circle above her head as she tried desperately to retain her balance. Dark water loomed below in the gap between the wall and the boat, and she tipped helplessly towards it.

'Julian . . .'

She cried out as she felt herself falling, and then hard hands grasped her wrists, and her arms were pulled almost from their sockets as the consultant stretched himself upright, dragging Berry with him up on to the safety of the walkway.

'Of all the stupid, irresponsible things to do. You might have been killed!' he growled. 'I told you . . .'

His face was tight with anger, and his hands gripped her arms as if he was about to shake her. Berry flared, 'I don't have to do as . . .' and then stopped as the *Crier* journalist clambered up from the deck to join them.

A quarrel between herself and Julian would destroy the image of their day out, whatever the reality might be, and she clamped her lips together to stop the angry words that tried to escape them, and turned to sort out her equipment, ready for its transfer to the boot of the Jaguar.

Her near-miss had shaken her more than she was prepared to admit. Instead of rescuing her, Julian might have had the unenviable task of trying to piece her together again, if he had not grabbed her in time, which would have given the reporter headlines of a very different sort for his next edition.

Berry shivered.

Julian said to the man amiably, 'Can I give you a lift back?' and the reporter answered, 'No, thanks. I'll get this copy into the office right away. It's only a step away along the harbour. If you'll just pose for me with Miss Baker and the skipper first, so that I can get a shot of you all with the boat in the background . . .'

Berry hoped that her smile as she posed beside Julian mirrored none of her true feelings. And, after thanking the two fishermen for their help, she waited impatiently while Julian stowed away the gear and let her into the Jaguar.

Thank goodness, the ill-starred day was over! Another half an hour, and she and the recording gear would be safely in the studio , and she could forget the whole sorry episode.

Julian keyed the engine into life and the car nosed its way off the hard, pointing, Berry saw, in the opposite direction from the hospital.

'Where are you going?' she demanded sharply. 'It's time we went back. You've had your day out.'

'I paid for a whole day. Only half of it has gone, yet.'

Berry's suppressed anger spilled over. 'You're determined to get your money's worth, aren't you? Why did you let the reporter go, if you want still more?' The prospect of Julian's sole company for the rest of the day was not to be endured. 'Let's go back for him. He can get extra copy from the rest of the day. There's no point in giving him half a story.'

'What he's got already will be all good publicity for the ward fund. That's the reason he came in the first place.'

'Or were you afraid of your reputation, if you were seen out alone with me?' Berry jeered, striving in vain to goad him into turning the car back.

'That was uncalled for.'

'Why? You didn't pull your punches last night, when you followed me into the studio. You made your opinion of me very plain.'

'After you rushed out, John told me how the auction idea started.'

'So now you're prepared to overlook my part in it? Generous of you.'

'I'm not prepared to overlook what the students did. The next time I meet up with them, I'll put them straight on a few points of gentlemanly behaviour.'

'You'll do nothing of the kind. It's none of your business. *I'm* none of your business. Anyway, were *you* such a saint, when you were a student?'

It was hitting below the belt, and Berry knew a qualm of conscience. From what Trish had told her, Julian must have been already married while he was still a student.

She wriggled uncomfortably in her seat, but the words could not be unsaid. She cast a surreptitious glance at Julian, and saw the knuckles of his hands gleam suddenly white on the steering wheel, but when he spoke, those betraying knuckles were the only indication of the iron control behind his even words.

'As chairperson of the committee, you *are* my

business, while you're working to fund the ward I need. So, shall we call a truce, and enjoy the rest of the day out together? It won't be a particularly long one. I fly out tonight by the evening plane, so your obligation will be at an end by mid-afternoon at the latest.'

In spite of his suggestion to call a truce, his voice was harsh, and Berry wondered whether it was because she had hurt his pride by making it plain she did not want his company, or because she had stirred memories of his student days, when he had been married to Kathleen.

Julian was responsible for resurrecting her own unhappy memories, so in that respect they were quits, she told herself, but a lingering conscience made Berry concede grudgingly, 'If you insist. Where are we going?'

'To that pub along the coast, for lunch. I told you about it the other day, when we went to the warehouse. You'll like it. It's an old smugglers' haunt.'

Berry was prepared not to like either the pub or the lunch that followed, and was irritated to find herself charmed by the one and enjoying the other.

They had to leave the car and walk down a steep track, to where the small building nestled at the entrance to a tiny, hidden cove.

'Not many tourists find their way here, because of the rough walk.' Julian reached out and grasped Berry's hand to help her, as she jumped down a particularly steep part.

She landed, and looked up at him, and her breath suddenly caught in her throat as his eyes scoured her face for what seemed an eternity before he turned and added abruptly, 'The rest of the way is smoother.'

In spite of that, he kept a firm hold on her hand, and without resorting to an undignified struggle it was impossible to pull away. Berry excused her uncharacteristic dependence upon his help on the still difficult walking, and used the same excuse for her accelerated heartbeat when they slid together, laughing and floundering on the foot-trapping shingle, to the pub entrance.

'How did you find it?' Berry marvelled as she walked unimpeded through the low doorway, and Julian jack-knifed his long length under the low lintel to follow her. 'I've been in Aldermouth for several years now, and I've not been here before.'

'It's a regular stopping-off place for the fishing-smacks and the yachting fraternity. They provide nearly all the trade.'

'It would be a riot in the middle of London, with food as good as this.' Berry savoured the delicate prawns, served with a wine sauce, with astonished appreciation. 'When the smugglers went away, they must have left their chef behind.'

'She isn't French. She's a local woman, the wife of the landlord. I can't imagine she would be happy in London. Is that where you hailed from, before you came to Aldermouth?'

It was casually asked, almost indifferently, and Julian's eyes remained attentive on his plate, not looking at her as he spoke. So was it only her own hypersensitivity that made Berry suspect his attention was sharper on her answer than he would have her believe?

She dismissed the thought as pure fancy, and allowed guardedly, 'I never had a real base until I came to Aldermouth. Unless you can call being pushed from one boarding-school to another a base. After that, I lived for a while in the south before I came to work here.'

Not London. Not specifically anywhere. Just, in the south. Nowhere that Julian could identify, if he wished to be curious.

'No family?'

'Only a crabby guardian, and the moment I came of age he washed his hands of me. What about you?'

Berry asked the question in order to side-track Julian from asking any more himself, but suddenly she found herself shrinking from what his answer might be.

Would he tell her about his wife? Hope and dread warred in her mind, leaving her confused and bewildered, because Julian's past, and his present, were nothing to do with her.

The thought brought with it a strange blankness, but before she could examine it he answered, 'My parents are both dead, and you know I lost Kathleen, my wife.'

'I'm sorry.' It sounded stiff and insincere, but what else could she say?

'It was a long time ago. Nothing can take away the happy hours.'

From what Trish had told her, he made them a shrine. A one-woman man . . .

He went on, 'I still have a sister and a half-brother left. Mary lectures on economics. She's in America at the moment. I hope to see her while I'm over there. Tom's into law, and he's welcome to it. It's too devious a profession for me, but he seems to thrive on the mental challenge of unravelling other people's tangled lives.'

Julian's tone was easy, and his smile seemed completely unforced as he spoke about his family, past and present. Slowly, the tension drained out of Berry, and she agreed readily enough when he suggested,

'Shall we walk our lunch down? The cove's lovely.

The beach is sandy further along. The shingle stops just past the pub.'

Julian lifted Berry over the sliding heaps of stones and set her feet down on firm sand, which was still damp from the receding tide. A shiver akin to excitement ran through her as his hands circled her waist, and she blamed it on the unaccustomed glass of lunch-time wine and the freshening breeze that blew straight in from the sea, tangling her hair and blowing it into her eyes, so that she could not see clearly.

Tangled lives.

His description teased at Berry's mind. Tangled was exactly what her own life had been, and for a long time she had found it impossible to unravel the knots and come to terms with what was left and attempt to see her way clearly. But that was over now, with only the scars left to throb, now and then, to remind her.

Abruptly, Berry spun to face the wind, turning her back on Julian and sending her hair streaming out behind her, clearing her vision, and straightening out this tangle more easily than she had been able to straighten out the other.

With a quick tug, she knotted her scarf over her head, subduing the tossing strands, and said brightly, 'I feel a bit like Robinson Crusoe, leaving my footprints on the sand.'

'The next tide will wipe them away, ready for some new ones tomorrow.'

If only life would be so kind, and erase the past, leaving no trailing mists of memory to cloud the days that followed. The thought passed like a straying cloud across Berry's face, and to hide it she bent swiftly, and plucked at a strand of seaweed, dislodging it from a dark mat lying on the shore.

She swung her booty to and fro between them with a careless-seeming abandon as she planned, 'I'll hang it out of my window, to forecast the weather.'

Julian reached down and took the other end, making the bubbly brown strip a link between them.

'It must only forecast fair weather for you, or it will have to answer to me.'

Berry turned startled eyes to look at him. The second he took it up, the seaweed became alive with a vibrant electricity that seemed to burn her fingertips. Her hand jerked sharply, and her fingers moved to open and drop her end, and found they could not.

Some strange magnetic current welded her finger-ends to the innocent conductor, binding her to Julian through its short, drab length. It held her with a strength no shore-plucked strand of seaweed ought to show.

In Julian's hold, it developed a magic property that sent the blood racing through her veins with a heady mixture of excitement and fear, that galvanised her feet, and sent her racing across the sands, with no clear idea of where she was racing to, or what she was racing from.

Julian ran too, keeping pace with her easily, although Berry's shorter legs were running as fast as they could. Still the strand of seaweed lay like a manacle between them, until he swung his arm and snapped it free, tossing it so that it sank slowly in the clear, shallow mirror of a rock pool, which had been left by the tide.

Berry flung herself down panting on the sand, beside the tiny sheet of trapped water, and Julian leaned across it beside her and said, 'Let's look for crabs.'

'I thought you had to go into deep water to find crabs, like the ones we caught this morning.'

Crabs were a nice safe topic of conversation, to help

quell the sudden turmoil that boiled up inside her—from where, she could not guess.

'Those are the big ones. The baby ones often get caught in the rock pools when the tide turns, and have to wait for the next one to wash them back into the sea. They're fun to find. Didn't you ever go crab-hunting on holidays when you were small?'

Berry's holidays had been bleak times of loneliness, incarcerated in an otherwise empty school. Afterwards, when the other girls returned at the beginning of another term, talking about the fun they had had with their families, she tried to tell herself she did not care, but the hurt remained just the same.

She evaded, 'I've never hunted for baby crabs. Show me.'

They bent together over the rock pool; the two reflected faces, side by side, gazed back at them from the water, and Berry drew back hurriedly and said,

'I thought I saw something move. There, in that corner. Is it a crab?'

The movement she saw was the reflection of Julian's face turning towards her own, and nervously she jerked away. For a long moment, the reflected green eyes continued to hold her, looking up from the depths of the pool, and then the placid surface was shattered as Julian dived his hand into the water, not towards the corner where she had pointed, but into the centre.

He drew it out, dripping, and clutching a tiny crustacean that waved its claws in miniature menace at this monstrous thing that invaded its hiding place

Julian held it out towards Berry. 'He's cute, isn't he?'

Berry cringed away as the crab, deciding it had had enough of being suspended in mid-air, began to sidle sideways on Julian's hand.

'Don't drop it. Don't . . .'

Another half-inch, and the crab would drop off his hand and straight into her lap. Julian loomed over her, his green eyes laughing at her panic.

'He won't hurt you. He's too tiny to be able to pinch.'

'Take him away! He's just like a spider. I hate spiders.'

For a brief, terrified second, Chris was back, tormenting her with spiders. Berry's nerve broke. She gained her feet in an undignified scramble, and fled. Anger lent wings to her heels, furious anger against Julian for tormenting her, and her one desire was to put as much distance as possible between him and the crab, and herself.

She heard him call out, 'Berry!' And again, '*Berry!*' This time it was on a harder, impatient note, and then he was on her, and his arms caught her and drew her to a halt.

'Let go of me! Don't touch me! Take the crab away!'

Hysterically, she fought to free herself. In the struggle, the knot of her headscarf came undone, and the wind laughed and whisked it away over the cliff.

Automatically, she grabbed at it, but she was too late, it had gone beyond recall. Since it was a scarf which Chris had given to her, she let it go without regret, glad to be rid of this last of his presents.

More urgent was the crisis that threatened her now. She turned shrinking eyes on Julian's hands. Which one held the crab?

'I haven't got the crab. For goodness' sake, I'm not a callous child, to use one creature to torment another.' His hands shifted to Berry's shoulders and gave her a quick, hard shake. 'The crab's back in the pool, where it belongs.'

'Promise?' Long shudders still shook her.

'Honestly.' Julian loosed one hand at a time, and held them, palms facing her to show her that there was no crab.

'I hate s-spiders. Anything that looks like a spider . . .'

Her words came jerkily, and she was unable to control her trembling. Julian's hands circled her, and pulled her close against him.

'You should know me better by now than to think I'd play such a cruel practical joke.'

She did not want to know him better. She hated what little she *did* know of him. But one of his arms trapped her, and the same inexplicable sense of excitement and fear flowed from his touch as the fingers of his other hand played with her hair.

'You've lost your scarf,' he discovered.

'It was an old one. It doesn't matter.'

It mattered that her hair crackled with the electricity of his touch. Berry could feel her scalp tingle as the strands stood erect, clinging to his fingers as he held his hand suspended for a moment above her head. The primeval sensation of warning shocked Berry into action, and she stammered urgently, 'It's time we went back. You said mid-afternoon. It's nearly that now. Your plane . . .'

Her words came out, disjointed, on a sudden shortness of breath that must have been caused by the steep cliff path up which she had run.

'We've still got nearly an hour yet before I need to go.'

'John hasn't,' Berry countered swiftly, and ad libbed with an inspiration born of desperation, 'He'll want the recording equipment back.'

'What recording can he possibly do on a Sunday afternoon?'

'He takes the mike round the wards to get requests from patients and relatives during the visiting hour.'

That could be done on any day of the week, but Julian was unlikely to know that.

'He didn't say anything about it when I borrowed the gear last night.'

'He'd expect me to remember, and return it in good time. If we don't, it'll upset the whole of our broadcasting schedule, and disappoint the patients.'

It was the only point of blackmail on which Julian might be vulnerable, and Berry used it without compunction, gloating inwardly when she saw him hesitate.

'You can't disappoint the patients.' She turned the screw, and saw his eyes suddenly narrow, telling her that he was not entirely convinced.

His arms tightened round her, instead of letting her go, and she stiffened against their hold as he said softly, 'By the same token, you mustn't disappoint me. I bid a high price for the day out with you.'

His head lowered above her. Her wide eyes saw it like a bright sun, blotting out the sky. She had to do something, quickly, before it eclipsed her.

Before his arms could tighten any further and trap hers between them, she pulled them free and raised her hands to cover her lips, crying through their shelter, 'You've already had what you bid for. A day out in my company.'

'Officially, it isn't finished yet.'

His lips hovered dangerously close, the hard set of them threatening the frail defence of her fingers.

Berry's eyes grew wild in her upturned face, and the

fear was paramount now, overriding the excitement in her veins as she cried, 'So far as I'm concerned, the day's already over. It's finished, do you understand? If you don't think the price was worth it, it's your own fault. You shouldn't have bid so much.'

'I'm not complaining about the price.'

'But you expected . . . favours? Is that it?'

The loathsome word was out, and she saw Julian's face go white, but she did not care. She had neither forgotten, nor forgiven, his earlier sneer, and the acid of it bit in her voice as she flung his words back into his face.

'Only one favour. This.'

He took his favour from her mouth, his lips extracting a punishing toll that pressed hers apart on a wordless cry of protest. When it was over, he thrust her away from him, and Berry staggered back and stared at him with eyes that were a blur of smoky hazel, while she pressed shaking hands, which had been helpless moments before, over her mouth.

'Call it a parting favour,' Julian mocked her distress, 'on account of the fact that I'll be gone before the end of the day.'

# CHAPTER SEVEN

THE days after Julian left held an unaccountable blankness that Berry was at a loss to identify.

She was hectically busy. She was on demand to open bazaars, appear at coffee mornings, acting as starter to marathons, and even taking part in one herself. All this, on top of her routine work at the studio, doing broadcasts and ward interviews, meant she had not a moment to herself.

Structural work on the new ward was progressing apace, and Berry added interviews with the workmen as extra-interest programmes and took it upon herself to sift the entries for the crayoning competition that flooded in daily from the small outpatients, as well as from those in the wards.

John teased her, 'If you go on at this rate, you'll soon have enough money to build a whole new hospital, never mind a single ward.'

'I'm enjoying it,' Berry defended, and redoubled her efforts.

When Julian returned, she was determined to show him that she had not dragged her feet. She would show him that she could cope, without his help, with all that the campaign could throw at her in the way of work and organisation.

In spite of her efforts, however, Julian's absence left an emptiness that all her frenzied activities were unable to fill. It was like the void in the eye of a storm and, no matter how hard Berry drove herself, there remained a flatness about her days that refused to go away.

Julian's latest kiss on the cliff path above the cove had left an indelible impression upon her lips that no amount of furious soaping was able to erase, and his charisma had left an equally indelible impression upon her senses.

If he had come into her life immediately after Chris, she could have blamed the force of his attraction as coming on the rebound. But Chris was a long way into the past and, apart from a few scars, she now held the reins of her life firmly in her own hands.

She was, nowadays, confident, mature . . . and still vulnerable, she discovered uneasily.

The effects of her long hours of working began to show in rings of weariness smudging her eyes, and Trish taxed her with it one night when Berry dropped in for her accustomed cup of coffee in the ward office, a habit she had resumed now there was no longer any chance of Julian coming to join them.

'We're almost half-way to our target,' Berry gloated.

'That's fine, but don't overdo things.' Trish cast her a professional glance. 'You're looking absolutely whacked.'

'I joined the Boy Scouts on a sponsored hike yesterday, and they walked me off my feet.'

Night did not bring her the expected rest, and Julian's voice pursued her into sleep, not telling her this time to raise the money, but shouting angrily, 'Favours? It depends on how far you're prepared to go.'

Berry raised her hands to strike at him, and awoke fighting the bedclothes. She worked off the nightmare by taking the entries from the crayoning competition to the skipper of the *Harbour Belle*, and handing them to him to choose the winner.

'Mr Vyse not back yet, then?' the fisherman

observed, and Berry shook her head, as much to shake it clear of Julian's lingering image as to answer her questioner.

Clearly, if the consultant had been back, the fisherman expected the two of them to be together, and hastily Berry set out to erase the assumption with a careless, 'He'll be back some time. I've got no idea when.'

She knew in that moment that she had missed him.

As you miss an aching tooth after it's been taken out, she jeered at herself, but no amount of self-deception could alter the unpalatable fact. It was disturbing, incomprehensible, and totally humiliating, and it dogged her at every turn.

So when Trish suggested to her later, 'Come and have supper with Alan and me tomorrow. I'm off duty for a couple of nights,' Berry accepted with alacrity.

In Trish's company, she would be able to escape from her own thoughts. She could not share her feelings with the ward sister. Trish would not understand them, any more than she understood them herself, but the other girl's lively chatter would help to keep them at bay.

At least going there to supper would get her visit over before Julian returned to make the party a foursome, she thought thankfully.

Trish told her, 'Come casual,' and Berry donned gold cord slacks and a gold sweater with a deep roll-neckline, and was lounging on the rug, listening to the ward sister's records when the telephone rang.

'I'll take it. I'm nearest,' Trish called from the kitchen, and a moment later the receiver clicked and Berry heard her exclaim, 'That's great! Yes. Plenty.'

The receiver clattered back on to its rest, and Trish hurried back to her post beside the stove, but she proffered no explanation of the call.

Berry called through to her, 'Is there anything I can do to help?'

But Trish answered cheerfully, 'Stay where you are, and stick your feet up for a change. You deserve it, after all the running about you've been doing. Alan will be back in a few minutes, with a bottle of plonk. But there's nothing posh. Its a sit-where-you-feel-like, pick-as-you-please feed tonight. I thought we could keep the records going, and eat round the fire.'

Trish hummed happily to the Ivor Novello oldie, and Berry heard a spoon stir busily in a saucepan, while its owner's voice gathered lilac in the springtime.

She stretched her legs luxuriously across the rug, and leaned back against the arm of the settee, and a drowsy feeling of relaxation pervaded her as she listened to the music with half-closed eyes.

She heard the front door of the flat open and close. That would be Alan with the plonk. Berry smiled, but she did not move. She was as at ease with Alan as she was with Trish, and she did not need to stand on ceremony with either of them.

'... until our hearts have learned to sing again,' crooned the recorded voice, when other, deeper masculine tones cut across the music with an appreciative,

'Novello doesn't date, does he?'

The scent of Julian's aftershave lotion alerted Berry split seconds before he spoke. It put to flight the lovely relaxed feeling and set the adrenalin flowing, sending needles of warning to prick every nerve-end in her body.

Her eyes flew open, and Julian's mouth curved in a smile as he looked down at her and said, 'You look like a kitten, curled up on the rug like that. I want to stroke you.'

He dropped on to the settee behind her, and Berry sat

bolt upright, away from her leaning-post, and drew her
legs under her, ready to jump to her feet.

'Stay where you are. There's no need to disturb
yourself.'

He was disturbing her more than a little, but it was not
in the way he meant. His hand came down on her
shoulder, drawing her back to her former position, but
where the upright of the settee had been his legs now
rested, and twin uprights of hard muscle replaced the
soft upholstery behind her, pressing against her back in a
way that threatened to melt her spine.

The fingers of his other hand passed over her head in a
sensuous, stroking motion that would have made a
kitten purr. It sent Berry's mind winging back to the
cliff path out of the cove, and . . .

She exploded away from him to the other side of the
rug, and crouched, staring up at him, her eyes smoky,
and her every nerve taut, like a wild creature, unsure
whether to run or to stay and fight.

'What's the matter? Don't you like being stroked?'

'I . . . you . . . it musses my hair.'

He watched her lazily, his eyes deep green and
inscrutable in the flickering shadows from the log fire
that Trish declared was her very nicest luxury and worth
all the work that it entailed.

'I've brought you something back that will keep it in
order.'

Julian reached into his pocket, and drew out a tissue-
paper packet. He stretched a long arm across the rug,
and Berry shrank back, keeping out of his reach.

For a moment his arm stilled, and he directed a long,
level glance at her before he remarked, 'It won't bite.'

He dropped the package into her lap, and Berry stared
down at it, making no attempt to peel off the wrappings.

'What is it?'

She had no fear of the package. It was the giver who caused her pulse to race, and her mouth to thirst for a glass of Alan's plonk to quench its sudden dryness.

'Open it and see.'

'Have you got a present? Let's all see.' Trish bustled in, followed by Alan, and they crowded round, looking down, waiting for Berry to open the tissue paper.

An odd kind of paralysis gripped her fingers, and the fire felt suddenly much too hot, making her hands slippery as she parted the wrapping and lifted up the silk square inside it for them to see.

'Ooh, pure silk! Sheer indulgence,' Trish sighed enviously. 'I love the colours.'

It was like holding a rainbow in her fingers. A faint current of air from the living-room fire stirred the delicate material, making the vivid pattern come alive, and Berry stared down at its beauty, stunned.

The scarf must have cost a fortune.

She did not know what to say. She could not find her voice to say anything at all. Her silence impinged, and Julian asked, 'Are the colours right for you?'

'Y-yes. They're lovely. Th-thank you,' Berry stammered.

Julian explained to the others, 'Berry lost her other scarf on the cliffs, when we had the day out together after the auction.'

Trish's eyes twinkled. 'Oh, yes?' she grinned, and Berry groaned inwardly.

Why did Julian have to give her the scarf here, of all places? Why did he have to give her the scarf at all?

Losing her other scarf had been like the snapping of the last link between her old life and her new. Before she had time to taste her freedom, this other scarf, like a delicate manacle, arrived out of the blue, threatening to trap her again.

'Try it on,' Trish urged. 'Let's see how the colours look on you.'

There was no help for it. Reluctantly, Berry draped the scarf over her head. It whispered across her shining brown bob like the touch of Julian's fingers stroking her hair. The softness of the silk caressed her cheek, warm as the warmth of his breath when he kissed her.

With a muffled exclamation, Berry pulled the square free, making a hasty excuse, 'It's too hot in the house to wear it. I'll wait until I go home.'

It seemed, to Berry's stretched nerves, as if that time would never come. Trish's carefully prepared buffet, and Alan's wine, left not the slightest impression upon her, although conversation flowed freely enough.

Julian refused to discuss his lecture tour at any length, merely commenting, 'I managed to meet up with my sister. We had a grand day out together at the beginning of the tour and then we had to go in opposite directions.'

When Trish begged 'Tell me about the lectures,' he shook his head, smiling, and said, 'I won't bore Berry and Alan with the medical details. I'm preparing a paper on the tour for the students. I'll let you have a copy of it, to read at your leisure.'

'Some leisure,' Berry snorted.

Trish shot back with a telling, 'You can't talk. You've worked yourself into the ground for the ward fund these last few weeks.'

'Bring me up to date,' Julian demanded. Nothing loath, Berry took full advantage of the opportunity.

She recounted with relish the multitude of activities she had master-minded during his absence, and Julian listened, but, she noticed vexedly, he listened with the same elusive expression of reserve on his face that had been there at the first committee meeting.

He failed lamentably to respond as she expected him to, when she announced triumphantly, 'The mayor's coming into the studio tomorrow evening, to announce the half-way figure to our target.'

She waited.

Surely, now, Julian would have the grace to admit that she had managed superlatively well without him? He opened his mouth to speak, but the congratulations she waited for did not emerge.

'While Prentiss is at the hospital, convene a meeting of the whole committee,' he instructed her briskly. 'I want to talk to them.'

'*You* want . . . I like that!' Berry erupted. 'I've worked myself to a standstill, and all you can say is . . .'

'That's exactly what I want to talk about,' Julian retorted, and refused to be drawn any further, firmly cutting across Berry's protests with, 'We'll discuss it all together at the meeting,' before adamantly changing the subject.

The talk became general and, when Berry insisted upon helping Trish to wash up the dishes soon afterwards, the ward sister teased her in the privacy of the kitchen, 'I'm not sure it's safe to let you handle my supermarket best. You looked ready to break a plate over Julian's head out there.'

'He's the most arrogant, insufferable, self opinion-ated . . .'

And to think she had actually deluded herself that she had missed him!

'He's given you quite the loveliest scarf I've ever set eyes on. Don't forget to wear it when you go home, to show him you're grateful.'

'I don't feel grateful, right now.'

Defiantly, Berry carried the scarf in her hand when she bade Trish and Alan goodnight. Julian took his leave of them at the same time, and Berry told him shortly, 'I've come in my own car.'

'I know. I parked mine just behind it.'

A canopy of polished stars greeted them as Julian walked with her to her car, and Berry shivered and hunched into the collar of her coat against the threat of frost to come.

'There's no point in having a scarf if you don't wear it to keep you warm.'

Julian reached down and took the fine silk from her hand, and turned her to face him. With deft fingers, he draped the scarf over her head and knotted the ends under her chin. Berry shivered again, and this time it was not the chill air which caused it, but his touch.

Confused, she fumbled in her coat pocket for her car key, eager to be gone. But, instead of releasing her to open the door, Julian cupped her face in both his hands, and enquired softly, 'Did you miss me, while I was away?'

Yes, would be the truth, but she would die rather than admit it. And, if she did, it would not be the whole truth.

What *was* the whole truth?

Even to herself, Berry could not give an answer. The blankness in her days since Julian went had been there before he came on the scene, yet she had not noticed it before.

She did not notice his hands move until it was too late to pull away. They crept round to the back of her head, gliding smoothly across the fine silk of the scarf, until they met and tipped up her face to meet his lips.

Berry knew a swift thankfulness that Trish and Alan

had gone back indoors and would not see, and then knew nothing more for a long moment as, impatient at her refusal to answer his question, Julian sent his lips to seek an answer for themselves.

Absence had done nothing whatever to lessen his impact. Her senses leapt to respond, and as their lips met, and merged, a shock-wave of feeling shuddered through her body.

While her mind cried a warning, her feminine instincts clamoured to meet him kiss for kiss, with a fervour that was a warning in itself. Julian felt her response, and his kiss changed, and deepened.

'Have you missed me?'

His lips punctuated each word, stroking down the slender column of her throat below the knot of the scarf, parting the collar of her coat, to come to rest in the perfumed hollow at the base, where a pulse throbbed wildly in response.

'I've ... been ... busy ...' Berry mumbled.

Her mind was incapable of remembering with what. The seeking lips crept on, creating a havoc inside her brain. Trapped in the circle of his arms, she felt her body begin to melt against him.

Was this what she had missed? The feel of his arms circling her? The touch of his lips against her skin?

'Evening sir, miss ...'

Measured footsteps plodded into Berry's consciousness. Julian straightened, and answered calmly, 'Good evening, Constable,' and Berry felt a hysterical urge to laugh as surely the last beat constable left in town tried the doors of the Jaguar.

Julian reassured him, 'That's my car. I'm going as soon as I've seen the young lady off.'

'Have a safe journey, both of you.'

Berry left it to Julian to answer. She felt incapable of coherent speech. With fumbling fingers, she unlocked the car door and dived inside, hiding her scarlet cheeks in the dark interior. The policeman remained where he was, conscientiously trying the doors of the other cars parked nearby, and his close proximity acted as the perfect deterrent to prevent Julian from trying to kiss her again.

Berry felt she could have hugged the officer of the law, and wondered, with an inward grin, what he would do if she tried. Julian leaned down to the car door, and she opened her window the merest crack, and kept her hand on the winder in case he should try to push it down further.

However, all he said was, 'See you at the committee meeting tomorrow. Let my secretary know what time.' He straightened, and raised his voice. 'Don't forget to switch your headlights on.'

In her confusion, Berry had forgotten, and it did not help that Julian should be the one to remind her. She almost felt as if she would have preferred it to be the constable, issuing a stern reprimand.

Car lights seemed superfluous. Her whole body felt as if it was ablaze with an inferno, ignited by Julian's kiss! She despised her own weakness in responding, and hated him for taking advantage of it. She drove mechanically, her brain in a turmoil.

Her frame of mind was no calmer the next evening, when she made her way to the matron's office where the committee meeting was due to be held. Stubbornly, she refused to hold it in Julian's office, and thus give him the initial advantage.

Her day had gone badly. An electrical fault had put the microphone out of order, and a flood of complaints from her disappointed listeners had kept the studio phone ringing before she'd managed to get it repaired. Her nerves felt ragged as she prepared to do battle if Julian should try to criticise the efforts of herself and the rest of the committee since he had been away.

They were waiting when she walked through the door, and Berry tensed as the consultant's eyes lanced across the room to her, but she thrust aside her nerves and announced brightly, 'Julian asked me to bring us all together, to discuss the fund-raising activities. I can't think why, unless it's to congratulate everyone on their hard work,' she added sweetly, returning his look with one that was quite the reverse.

Before Julian could respond, Matron cut in with, 'I've got the latest figures here from some more events that have been held in the town.' She smoothed out the paper in her hand and read, 'WI sale of work, fifty pounds. Scouts' sponsored hike, one hundred and eighty, and a jumble sale, seventy-five.'

'That's wonderful.'

'It's chicken-feed.'

Every eye in the room turned to Julian, amid a shocked silence. He was on his feet, his hands planted firmly on the top of Matron's desk, and a look of unrepentant scorn on his face. 'Chicken-feed,' he repeated deliberately.

'How dare you criticise the amounts?' Berry blazed. She, too, stood to face him, and their eyes locked in battle across the heads of the other members of the commitee. 'You're not even on the committee. You've got absolutely no right ...' Her words choked on her outrage.

'My work at the hospital gives me the right.'

'We've already raised half of the money we need.'

'We can't afford to relax until we've got it all, and unless it arrives in much bigger quantities than those that Matron's just read out, people will get tired of fund-raising before we've reached our target. We must raise the money quickly, because prices are rising all the time.'

'Everyone's worked themselves to a standstill! You haven't seen all the effort that's been put into getting the chicken-feed, as you call it. You've been away, doing your own thing.'

'If I hadn't had to go away, I would have intervened earlier.'

'To do what?'

'To stop you all from wasting your efforts on . . .'

'Chicken-feed?' The words seemed to stick in her throat.

'I know that everyone has worked tremendously hard.'

'Big of you to admit it,' Berry flared.

Julian ignored her and pressed on, 'It's a pity that all the effort has been geared to running small events, when one big one would have achieved better results. Jumble sales are all very well in their place, but they won't pay the builders on time.'

'So, what do you suggest? We haven't got a magic wand.'

'I suggest we organise a gala day for the whole town.' The suggestion sounded more like an order, and Berry bridled, but before she could interrupt Julian continued, 'It's the end of season, and with the whole town *en fête* it would give a boost to the tourist trade, so the shopkeepers and hoteliers would be only too willing to go along with it.'

'That's a marvellous idea, Julian!' the mayor applauded. 'Why didn't we think of it before?'

Because Julian had not seen fit to mention it before. The unspoken reason seemed to echo like a knell in Berry's ears, as Julian warmed to his theme.

'We could approach the yacht club to hold a regatta, and get the various organisations in the town to decorate floats for a procession. There could be a firework display over the harbour. The fishing fleet would help out there. And a civic ball, and a town lottery.'

'With a brand new car as a prize, I suppose?' Berry slid in thinly.

'It could happen, if you'd beam your efforts in the right direction.'

Berry's efforts of late had drained her of time and energy, but until now she had thought the results to be worthwhile. At a stroke, Julian consigned them to trivia, and swept the board with a plan of his own.

With hindsight, Berry realised it must have been in his mind from the very first meeting, thus giving him plenty of time to think the details through.

With hindsight, she realised she should have thought of it herself. But she had not, and Julian had returned and taken charge once again. The eager discussion going on round her told her that the rest of the committee had basely transferred their allegiance, and she must go along with them, or be left out.

Berry refused to allow what was originally her idea to be taken over with such high-handed totality. With angry determination, she immersed herself in every possible detail of the arrangements that followed.

The weeks passed by in a blur of organising activity, and Julian seemed to be everywhere at once. Doggedly, Berry went along with him, step for step.

Like Man Friday, she likened her role with bitter

self-derision, but she stuck to her guns and to Julian's side, refusing to be left out of any single detail of what he was doing.

'Give yourself a break this weekend. You're looking tired out,' he told her abruptly one Friday evening, after a particularly arduous afternoon, but Berry curtly refused.

'I've got my second wind. I'm fine.'

He was not going to get rid of her so easily, and although her mind and her body longed for a break, she forced herself to endure yet another endless meeting of yet another sub-committee, determined to keep going until the bitter end, even if it killed her.

By the time the gala day finally arrived, Berry felt so weary that she reckoned it probably would, but the sight of a brand-new red Mini exhibited on a stand in the middle of the town square, with a long queue of people lining up to buy lottery tickets, rejuvenated her flagging energy.

'You managed to get a car, after all,' she congratulated the mayor, and had her joy blighted when he corrected, 'It was none of my doing. Julian charmed it out of a local dealer. Great, isn't it?'

Did he mean the Mini, or Julian? Berry shot the bright little runabout a look calculated to remove the shine from its bumpers, and turned her back on it, pretending to busy herself with her recording equipment.

The gala day would provide her with providential material for her broadcasts from the studio, but her intention to wander among the crowds on her own, taping whatever might be suitable, was doomed to swift disappointment.

Julian commandeered a supermarket trolley, loaded

the recording equipment on to it, and trundled it alongside her, overruling her protests that she could manage on her own, with a facetious, 'If you get too tired, you can jump on for a ride.'

During the last hectic weeks, Julian had dragged her along on a ride she was not likely to forget, and Berry longed for nothing so much as to jump off a wagon that seemed to be careering with increasing speed out of her control.

After that night outside Trish's flat, he had not attempted to kiss her again. Indeed, he had seemed to engineer matters so that they were rarely alone together.

There was nothing she could put her finger on, but Berry sensed that the engineering was deliberate, and told herself firmly that she was glad ... glad.

Once, at the end of a particularly long day, Julian had bent his head as if he might be going to kiss her, and then had seemed to change his mind and drawn back. Instead, he had said, in a constrained-sounding voice, 'Goodnight, Berry. See you tomorrow.'

And he'd turned away, leaving Berry feeling unaccountably deprived, and hungry with a hunger that could not be satisfied by food, and at a loss to account for either, considering her aversion to the consultant.

She thrust aside the conundrum as being too difficult to solve, and said, 'I'm going down to the harbour to record the winners of the crayoning competition. The skipper's taking them all out in the *Harbour Belle* this morning.'

It was a noisily cheerful gathering that would effectively take her mind off Julian's presence, too close beside her, his fingers brushing hers occasionally as they met amid the tangle of wires and plugs.

He said, 'At the last count, there were about twenty

children. The skipper's probably raked in a few more by now, to fill his boat. How many interviews do you want to get?'

'I'll just wander about among them, and let it happen,' Berry responded, wise in experience. 'Individual children tend to dry up when they're faced with the mike.'

'Let's be children too, just for today.' Unexpectedly Julian stopped, reached across the trolley, and caught Berry's hands in his, and his eyes held a curious appeal as he went on persuasively, 'We've done all the hard work. For the rest of the day, let's relax and have fun, like everybody else.'

The idea was irresistibly appealing.

The carnival atmosphere was infectious. Couples strolled arm in arm, and children shouted and laughed, and licked ice-cream and candy-floss. Suddenly, Berry knew that it had been too long since she had allowed herself a day off purely for pleasure.

But this was to be a day out with a difference. A day with Julian. Moments from their last day out together were still vivid in her mind, and warned her she was playing with fire to risk another.

'Come on, give yourself a break for once.'

Laughing green eyes enticed her, challenging her, and Berry hedged, 'I'll have to take the recording equipment along,' as if it was a shield she could fix between them.

'We'll make the recording fun, too.'

Julian was as good as his word. Joyously, he helped her to interview the passers-by, who responded to his charm with enough material for half a dozen broadcasts. In spite of herself, Berry's spirits lifted, and the microphone caught her laughter joining in with Julian's as they trundled the trolley gaily between them towards the harbour to join the skipper and his young artist guests on the fishing-smack.

Berry looked on in astonishment as Julian set about enjoying himself on the children's level the moment they got on board. He laughed and teased, swapped jokes with the older children, and drew the smaller ones, unresisting, on to his lap as the fishing-smack rolled gently, unsettling their balance when it left the harbour bar.

'You've got a way with the young ones, Mr Vyse,' the grandfather skipper remarked, and Julian smiled.

'They're all patients of mine, and they know me.'

It was evident that they liked him, too, and Berry looked on, fascinated, as he listened gravely, and with infinite patience, to a small boy's rambling account of his school football team's latest match.

This was a side to Julian she had never suspected. She knew he could be thoughtful—kind, even. She had seen evidence of that in his attitude towards his elderly housekeeper, but somehow she had never connected the dynamic surgeon with children, except as patients.

'They like you,' she voiced her astonishment.

'Because they know I like them. Don't you like children, too?'

The question seemed to be loaded with something she could not understand, reinforced by an elusive expression deep in his bright green glance that made Berry feel suddenly flustered.

'Of course.' She felt her cheeks grow warm and turned hurriedly away to hide them when a small boy begged,

'Let me push the button on your machine, miss, to make it hum like it did on the ward.'

'Go ahead. Press it once, like this, then let it go. That's the way.'

Berry steadied the small hand just recently freed from plaster, and held the microphone unobtrusively close to catch the delighted reaction of the young button-pusher. The moment passed, and soon the trip was over too, and they were back once more in the crowded streets. Berry wielded her microphone, getting spot interviews as they walked along together.

The streets were crammed with people who parted with great good humour to allow them and their trolley, full of equipment, free passage. But they closed together and blocked Berry's view when the decorated floats started to roll past, so she had to hold her microphone high above her head, hoping it might catch some sounds of interest that she could edit later on, from the procession she was not tall enough to see.

'Stand in the trolley. I'll hold on to you, so that you won't fall.'

Berry gave a startled gasp as Julian grabbed her, and lifted her high, and then her feet were inside the trolley, and Julian's arms were wrapped tightly round her, binding her to him as firmly as if he were a stake supporting a slender-stemmed tree.

From her high vantage point Berry now had a perfect view of the procession as it rolled past, but the impact of Julian's closeness destroyed her advantage.

Her heightened senses were vividly aware of him, of his arms moulding them together, his hands gripping her securely, and contrarily making her feel less secure than she had ever felt in her life before.

Her eyes persisted in straying from the moving pageant she had come to see, downwards, instead, to the sight of Julian's head, the deep auburn waves of his hair resting against her side at waist level.

The wheeled trolley shifted slightly, responding to her movement, and although Julian held her securely, instinct made Berry put out a hand to steady herself, and it came into contact with the nearest thing to her, his head.

Her fingers gripped in auburn waves, and found them thick and soft, and knew an urge to linger there. Feeling her touch, Julian looked up, and at her, and Berry hurriedly snatched her hand away, denying her fingers their wish, but not before his eyes had seen and taunted her confusion, guessing its cause.

The procession rolled in front of her, float upon decorated float, but afterwards Berry could not remember which was which, and was forced to confess her ignorance later to John, and search his photographs in order to make sure that her broadcast news feature would be accurate.

John teased her, as she knew he would, and Berry cursed the chemistry in her make-up that reacted with the potency of champagne each time Julian touched her, but she was as powerless to control it as she was to prevent it. With his quick intuition, Julian knew that, and took a fiendish delight in starting the effervescent bubbles rising in her blood at every opportunity.

'You look lovely when you blush.' He bent swiftly and kissed the tip of her nose deepening still further the rising colour in her cheeks, before he bore her off to indulge in real champagne with the winner of the regatta.

They remained on board the yacht for the victory trip across the harbour, and the wind brought the cheerful sounds of the onshore band to their ears, and whipped Berry's hair into a tangle, so that she thrust her hand into her slacks' pocket, and pulled out a scarf to control it.

The scarf Julian had given to her.

She felt his eyes sharpen on it, recognising his gift, and wished she had chosen any other scarf in her possession to bring out today.

Her fingers had searched it out from among all the others in her drawer, excusing their choice as being lighter, and just as warm as the woollen equivalents, and moreover capable of being folded into a much smaller size, to fit into her pocket.

'Don't lose that one overboard,' Julian warned her as Berry tied it on, and her fingers tied an extra, precautionary knot of their own accord, making her wonder why the prospect of losing Julian's scarf should bother her, when she had watched the scarf Chris gave to her be whisked away by the wind without a moment's regret.

But the pace of the expertly planned gala day left no time for introspection, and as the early dusk began to settle they took the recording equipment to the promenade to get the reaction of the crowds to the coming firework display.

The fishing fleet was to present it from a good distance out into the harbour, using the darkness of the sky and the sea as a backdrop, and the first rocket arced skywards as they reached the promenade.

The walkway itself was ablaze with lights, and they made their way along it stopping every now and then for Berry to talk to passers-by at random, and tape their comments.

'The show's great, but the wind's cold,' recorded one shivering couple, and Berry had to agree ruefully, 'It could be warmer.'

No sooner had she said it than she felt warmth surround her, and looked up, startled, as Julian settled his jacket across her shoulders.

The smell of good tweed enveloped her, mixed with sensuous overtones from Julian's aftershave lotion, and something else, elusive, but wholly unique to him, combining in a heady brew that set her blood on fire making her impervious to the cold.

'You'll want it yourself,' she protested, trying ineffectually to shrug away the jacket, but he retorted, 'Keep it on, I'm not cold,' and made sure she obeyed him with gripping fingers holding the tweed across her.

Without doing public battle, Berry was unable to free herself from its folds and, confusedly, she took refuge in her work. Quickly, she turned and thrust her microphone towards a nearby party of day-trippers.

'Can I have your views on the carnival? Are you enjoying your day at Aldermouth? Tell me ...'

She stopped abruptly, and her microphone wavered.

'Well, I never!' a woman exclaimed. 'If it isn't Berry Baker!'

She was middle-aged, heavily made-up and beringed, and she thrust her face towards Berry as if she had just uncovered hidden treasure.

'It's years since I've set eyes on you,' she cried.

'You must be mistaken.' Berry tried to move away, but the crowd pressed in front of her, and the trolley was at her back. She was trapped.

The woman was not mistaken. And it was exactly four years ago.

Berry remembered her face and, even more clearly, her voice, as if it were yesterday. The first sound of it transported her back to those dreadful weeks of the court case that had resulted in the annulment of her marriage to Chris.

The woman had been a neighbour when she and Chris had moved into their flat, and she had been a constant spectator in the public gallery during the whole of the hearing.

She and her companions had listened avidly to every sordid detail of Chris's marital adventures, and afterwards she had kept the agony cruelly alive for Berry by her spiteful gossip.

'I'm not mistaken. I'd know you anywhere. I never forget a face, do I?' she appealed to her companions.

Emboldened by their agreement, she turned on Berry with the venomous intent of a viper about to strike.

'Your ex must be due out of jail about now. Which of his wives is he going back to?'

# CHAPTER EIGHT

BERRY stared at the woman, stunned.

She had always known that, one day, she might be confronted by the life she had left behind her. But, as the years passed, the possibility had become more and more remote, until eventually it had slipped to the back of her mind. Which made it all the greater shock, coming out of the blue now.

She felt sick. It was like a nightmare come true! All the old feelings of guilt and shame flooded back to engulf her. She stole a glance at Julian. He was staring down at her, his face agate-hard, and his eyes dark green, almost black in the lamplight.

She remembered seeing them darken in just that way once before, on the day of the auction, when he had stormed after her into the studio and shouted at her, blaming her for the whole thing.

From the expression on his face, it was obvious he was blaming her again now, doubtless condemning her as 'the other woman', heedlessly wrecking another girl's marriage. Few though they were, the woman's words had told their own story. And Julian's look made it plain that he had drawn his own conclusions from them, to Berry's discredit.

How dared he blame her, without even hearing her side of the story? Suddenly, something seemed to snap inside Berry. Julian had no right to blame her. He had no right, even, to hear her story. What had happened in the past belonged between herself and Chris, and the other unfortunate women he had duped.

Just as the shame and the guilt alike belonged to Chris, and not to herself. Furiously, Berry swept both aside with a proud toss of her head, as if she was sloughing off the discarded skin of the old, insecure Berry.

Rockets whizzed and banged across the sky above her head, and with a defiant tilt of her small nose she fired her own version from ground level.

'Wouldn't you like to know?' she flung back at the heavily made-up face, and had the satisfaction of seeing the double chin drop. With a fierce satisfaction, she pressed home her attack. 'I've no doubt you'll make it your business to find out who Chris goes back to, and broadcast it to the whole neighbourhood, but you're welcome to my share of him, if that's of any help to you.'

With her head in the air she stalked past the speechless woman, and thrust her way into the crowd. She did not wait to see if Julian was following her. She did not care. She never wanted to set eyes on him again, either.

Her feet drove her angrily forward, heedless of which direction they took her in. The crowds milled about her, and she noticed one or two of the passers-by give her curious stares, but she ignored them and pressed on.

Soon, however, the sheer weight of numbers along the crowded promenade slowed her down and, as the first fire of her anger began to subside, reaction set in.

A shaky feeling that started in the pit of her stomach spread rapidly to her knees, and then to her legs, and she looked round urgently for somewhere to sit down.

A vacant bench-end invited, and she dropped on to it thankfully. Then a merry voice penetrated her daze.

'Where have you been all day? We haven't set eyes on you once.'

Trish's voice. Berry looked round, startled, to find Alan and Trish sitting next to her on the bench. The ward sister was eyeing her with the same curious look that she had noticed from the other passers-by, and a quick frown marred Berry's forehead.

Why should people think it odd if a girl chose to walk on her own? Just because other people were walking in pairs, it did not necessarily follow that she either wanted, or needed, companionship. She said briefly, 'I've been working. Making recordings for the studio.'

'I thought Julian was with you?'

'He's around.'

'I can't see him.' Trish peered this way and that into the crowd.

'He's behind me, somewhere. He'll catch up. He's got my recording equipment with him,' Berry remembered belatedly.

'I'd say that makes you quits. You're wearing his jacket.'

So that was why she had attracted such curious stares from the passers-by. Why Trish's eyes teased. Berry felt the blood rush up into her cheeks. She had completely forgotten about the jacket!

Now that she remembered, the cloth seemed to close round her shoulders like an extension of Julian himself, stifling her. She gave a muffled exclamation, and grabbed hold of the lapels to tug it free.

'Keep it on,' Julian commanded, 'or you'll feel the cold.'

Berry spun round. She had not heard the trolley come up behind her. The noise of the fireworks, and the chattering of the crowds, had drowned the clatter of the wheels, and she turned hard eyes on the surgeon.

'I'm warm enough without it.'

Anger against Julian, and something else she did not stop to define, sent a glow of heat through her body, resisting the cool breeze. Defiantly, she dropped the jacket on to the trolley, and told him, 'Wear it yourself if you want to.'

It lay like a gauntlet thrown between them, and their glances clashed above the well cut tweed. Seemingly unaware of the silent duel being waged in front of her, Trish enquired, 'Are you doing ward rounds this evening, Julian? If you are, you could take the recording equipment back to the studio with you, and we'll give Berry a lift home. It'll give her a bit more time to make herself pretty for the dinner and ball tonight.'

Berry felt as if she needed a lot of time, not to make herself look pretty, but to gather her wits together, and regain some of her poise, which Julian's sudden appearance had rocked off balance again.

Anger completed what the hectic day had begun, and she suddenly felt spent, and unable to face still more hours in Julian's company. His face remained set in stern, unsmiling lines, and it provided the last straw that made up Berry's mind for her.

'I'm not going to the dinner or to the ball.'

A stunned silence greeted her announcement, and then everyone began to speak at once.

'It'll be a fabulous evening. You simply can't miss it!'

'You must come, Berry. Everybody will be there.'

'Why not?'

The last from Julian, curt, incisive, and with a razor-edge to the question that demanded an answer. Berry racked her mind to find a plausible excuse.

'I—I'm tired out.' That, at least, was true. 'It's been a long day.'

'If you go home with Trish and Alan now, you'll have two hours in which to rest.'

Two long hours in which to dread the even longer ones to come. Vehemently, Berry shook her head.

'You *must* put in an appearance, at least for the dinner, and the start of the ball,' Julian insisted.

'No one will notice if I'm not there.'

'Everyone will notice, including the press. All the committee are sitting at the top table, along with the mayor and mayoress, and an empty chair will attract immediate attention. Do you want to make front-page headlines—again?'

The slight pause hurled the last word at her like a cudgel, and Berry flinched as it struck home. Julian was privy to information that Trish and Alan were not, and she knew he was not referring to the recent publicity, when her efforts on behalf of the ward fund attracted almost daily attention in the local newspapers.

With cruel deliberation, Julian had harked back to the day-tripper's sneer, and all that it embraced. Berry felt the blood drain from her face, not with fear any more, but with hatred of Julian.

The slight information he had gleaned about her past was enough to enable him to turn it into a lash, and he wielded it without mercy in order to drive her into going his way.

'I won't,' she mutinied.

Trish coaxed, 'Come home with us and stick your feet up. You'll feel differently when you've had a rest. The chance to put on a long evening dress is enough to rejuvenate any woman. Would that it came more often,' the ward sister mourned.

'I'll call for you at half-past seven,' Julian said, and Berry's eyes flashed, but he cut across her rising, 'I told you, I'm not . . .' with a deliberate, 'I'm bringing the mayor and his wife with me. His chauffeur is ferrying some elderly people who've helped with the fund-raising, so I'm collecting the Prentisses on my way in. If you still intend not to come, you can explain the reason to the mayor yourself.'

Julian had won.

It was beginning to seem inevitable, Berry thought raggedly. He out-manoeuvred, out-distanced, and out-smarted her at every turn and her nerves jangled as she turned her attention to dressing for the evening.

Her gown was an off-the-shoulder extravagance of deep turquoise silk, with silver embroidery, in which she knew she looked her best. Second-best would be a better description of what she felt like tonight, she decided without humour, critically regarding, with shadowed eyes, the pallor of her reflection as it stared back at her through the mirror.

It would have to do. She did not possess blusher, and she would simply have to hope that the warmth of the ballroom might bring back sufficient colour to her cheeks to deter comment.

A choker of crystals reflected the colours of her dress as she moved, catching the light from the silver bracelet which she wore above her elbow. A silver stole completed the picture, and by the time the hands of the clock stood at three minutes to half-past, she was as ready to go as she would ever be.

Contrary to Trish's prediction, the dress had done nothing to make Berry change her mind. A long soak in the bath had taken away the physical tiredness, but it hadn't improved the state of her feelings.

Every nerve in her body felt tight as she waited at the window, the better to espy the Jaguar the minute it entered the small close. Exactly at half-past, its lights illuminated the turning, and she felt the familiar acceleration of her pulse as it drew to a smooth stop outside the house.

Swiftly, she sped across the room, and down the stairs into the lobby, determined that Julian should not have the opportunity to come up the stairs to collect her, and gloat over making her change her mind.

She reached the pavement at the same time as he got out of the car, and his eyes glittered as they raked her from head to toe, nodding approval of the way she looked.

'Nice,' he murmured, in a taunting undertone that mocked her capitulation. Berry gritted her teeth as he opened the car door to let her into the front passenger seat.

She had no need to wait for the warmth of the ballroom to bring colour back to her cheeks now, and her mind despised the traitorous way her heart accelerated at his faint praise.

Hurriedly, she averted her eyes from his head as he bent to tuck her dress safely inside before closing the car door, lest the sight of it should accelerate her heartbeat even more, and betray her confusion to the mayor and mayoress, who were sitting in the back of the car.

On arrival at the town hall, the party split to mingle among the guests, and to Berry's consternation Julian remained glued to her side, as if, she thought furiously, having obliged her to come, he intended to see that she had no opportunity to slip away while he was not looking.

With his unusual colouring, he made a striking figure in his evening clothes, and Berry was acutely aware of the looks that darted in their direction as they moved among the crowd. Acutely aware of Julian beside her, lightly guiding her with his hand under her elbow, including her in his conversations.

No one reacted strangely when she spoke, so she must have found the right words somehow, although she was hardly conscious of what was said to her, or of her own replies. For some reason, her usual easy, hail-fellow-well-met approach to people, that stood her in such good stead in her work at the hospital studio, seemed to have deserted her tonight, and she felt stiff and awkward beside Julian's easy urbanity.

What on earth's the matter with me? she asked herself angrily, as he steered her to her seat at the top table. She discovered, to her chagrin, that it was placed next to his own, and much too close for her comfort.

The hall was packed, and the chairs were fitted tightly together, and if she had not come she felt convinced that one chair taken out of the crush would not have been noticed.

Each time she moved, one arm and shoulder brushed against Julian's jacket sleeve, and it was like leaning up against a live electric wire.

A waitress brought starters, and Berry chose soup as being the easiest thing to swallow on a throat that suddenly closed against food, and then immediately regretted her choice when she had to lean sideways towards Julian in order to allow the girl to ladle the scalding liquid into her bowl across the confined space between the chairs.

Julian's alert eyes took in the difficulty, and with a smile to the waitress he put his hand round Berry's waist, and drew her even closer towards him, pressing her up against his shoulder while the girl completed her task.

Berry felt herself go scarlet. It seemed as if every eye in the room must be watching her. The top table was raised on a slight dais to enable a speaker to be more readily heard and seen when the speeches began, and that went for everyone who sat at the table as well.

It was like sitting in a goldfish bowl, and Berry felt just as conspicuous, and could have slapped Julian for embarrassing her so publicly. As if the woman on the promenade was not enough for one evening! Her new-found immunity, that had made her impervious to the barbs of her old adversary, did not extend to the surgeon, she discovered.

The waitress passed on, and Julian released her. Berry dug her spoon savagely into her soup, and gasped as the hot liquid burnt her tongue, which nursed its pain, too sore to invent a deflating reply when Julian taunted, *sotto voce*, 'Glad you came, after all?'

Glad, because he had put his arm round her? His conceit was beyond all words! Berry glared at him wrathfully, and tried to ignore the wail of desertion that rose from the region of her waist, where Julian's hand had held her for a brief, palpitating moment, and now mourned its loss.

Abruptly, Berry turned away without answering, and forced her mind to fix itself on what the woman opposite to her at the table was saying.

'... my little granddaughter. She's only six. She's a little angel. She competed in one of the sponsored races we held for the ward fund, and won.'

To Julian, Kathleen was an angel. And no one could compete with an angel, even if they wanted to.

Did *she* want to?

Without warning, the question tracked across Berry's mind, like one of the rockets set off by the fishing fleet, and the answer burst upon her consciousness with an explosion that threatened to rock her mind off balance.

Yes, she did want to.

Even as the answer came, Bery knew despairingly that she could never hope to win. Julian was a one-woman man. And she, Berry, was not that woman.

Helplessly, she watched all the inexplicable moods and feelings of the last traumatic weeks fall into place, and stared with anguished eyes at the picture they presented.

Why did she have to fall in love with the two men in the whole of the world who could bring her nothing but unhappiness? First Chris, and now Julian.

Julian had no patience with people who made the same mistake twice. She had done just that, and would pay a bitter price. But Julian must never suspect.

Her love for Chris had been young, inexperienced, immature. First love, for her if not for Chris, flowering early, and fading soon. With experience, she knew that her love for Julian was different. It was a mature love, the kind of love to last. It explained the gap in her life that had so puzzled her when he had gone away, a gap that would always be there now, for the rest of her days, yawning wider because of her own bitter self-revelation.

Bleakly, Berry found herself praying that today's carnival would raise sufficient money to close the ward fund and disband the committee. Loving Julian, she could not bear to continue seeing him day in and day out for, if she did, how would she be able to hide her feelings from him?

If he should find out, his rejection would be worse than any humiliation Chris had managed to inflict upon her.

Julian was a one-woman man.

To him, Kathleen was an angel.

And no one could compete with an angel.

The words buzzed round and round in Berry's mind like a bee against a window-pane, striving to be set free, but she dared not speak them out loud. Dared not even allow herself to think them, for fear they might be written on her face, and Julian would read.

She nodded and smiled mechanically as the woman chatted on about her granddaughter, while her mind raced with plans. She would have to leave the studio. John would want to know her reason, and she would not be able to tell him, but somehow she would find an excuse, because she could not endure the daily possibility of bumping into Julian.

If she did, she could not guarantee that her secret would remain safe, and her pride shrank from his reaction if he should guess.

What applied to her work, also applied to her flat, Berry realised miserably. Julian had got into the habit of calling for her there and, if she was ever to know peace again, it must not continue. The flat, too, would have to be sacrificed on the same agonising altar that had taken her happiness before. Once again, she would have to uproot herself, and go somewhere else, and start all over again.

Was she doomed to be always a refugee from her own unhappiness?

The dinner dragged on. Speeches followed, congratulatory to Berry, and she gritted her teeth and pinned a smile on her face, longing for the evening to come to an end.

The mayor turned towards Julian and announced, 'We'll now ask Mr Vyse, who I'm sure I have no need to introduce to any of you, to draw the lottery ticket, and let us know who is the winner of the Mini.'

Life was a lottery, but so far none of the prizes seemed to have fallen into her lap, Berry thought bitterly.

Julian rose to his feet, smiling, and demurred, 'I'll concede the honour to Miss Baker. It was her idea in the first place to launch the ward fund. Without her, I doubt if any of this would have happened.'

Berry listened in astonishment. Julian was actually admitting, and in public, that the new ward was her idea, and her ears should have triumphed at his concession. Instead, they heard the words and dismissed them, because her mind was far too occupied with its latest crisis to care about their import.

Julian reached down a hand and drew Berry to her feet, and she went along with him, her mind in a daze, to where a large drum of tickets balanced on a spindle at the edge of the dais.

A handle protruded from one end, to enable it to be churned, and Berry gripped it and tugged, but its weight resisted her slender arms. 'I can't ...' she began urgently, and Julian came to her aid.

'Let me help you.' His hand closed over her own,

strong, and firm, and determined, and sent shocks of
awareness up her arm that paralysed her muscles,
rendering them useless, but he did not seem to be
similarly afflicted; obedient to his pull, the drum began
to revolve.

'There's no need for us both to turn it.' Ineffectually,
Berry tried to tug her hand free.

The feel of Julian's fingers circling her own on the
handle was doing demoralising things to her self-
control, and she felt herself begin to tremble, as the tears
that had lain only just underneath the surface during the
last fraught hours threatened to break through.

She must not break down here, in public, with half
the town looking on, but her frantic attempt to extricate
herself was fruitless. Julian's hand tightened in a grip of
steel, welding her fingers under his to the handle, and
turning them both remorselessly at his behest.

The constant circling became mesmeric, and Berry
felt panic begin to well up inside her, and knew how the
dancer in the red shoes must have felt when she had
discovered she could not take them off her feet and was
doomed to go on dancing in them for ever.

For ever was how it felt, before Julian finally decided,
'The tickets should be well shaken up by now.'

Shaken was a fair description of how Berry felt
herself, and dizziness seized hold of her as the drum
stopped, so that she was forced to hold on to the handle,
gripping it tightly in order to keep herself upright.

The background noise of conversation in the hall
became a roaring in her ears, and she was only vaguely
aware of Julian reaching up to open a small trapdoor in
the top of the drum. His voice seemed to come from a

long way away, telling her to, 'Reach in, and pull out a ticket.'

Her eyes could not see clearly where the trapdoor was, and her hand refused to let go of the handle. Berry sensed rather than saw Julian's look, suddenly keen, on her face, and frantically she shook off the threatening waves of darkness, blinked back the rising tears, and groped upwards blindly, guessing at where the trapdoor must be.

Again, lean fingers closed over her hand, this time guiding it into the depths of the drum, then letting it go and leaving her fingers bereft, to find a raffle ticket for themselves.

Numbly they scrabbled among the pile and latched on to one and, as she drew it out amid a waiting silence, a sudden desire to giggle rescued Berry. She gasped, on a note of half hysteria, 'He put in his thumb, and pulled out a plum.'

The words came out with a brittle gaiety, so brittle that her voice splintered with the effort of uttering them, and she had to hand over the ticket to Julian, for him to read out the name of the winner, because her own voice refused to function.

'Mr and Mrs Melland,' he called, and scanned the sea of upturned faces in front of them.

A deluge of applause broke out as a middle-aged couple got up from their seats, and hurried forward to receive the car keys from the mayor, and Berry's eyes blurred.

She did not envy the couple their prize. But how she envied them the closeness that automatically wrote their two names together, refusing to separate themselves even on so insignificant a thing as a lottery ticket.

A general exodus began towards the ballroom, and Berry and Julian were caught up among the crowd. People spoke to them, and expected to be answered, providing an antidote of normality that steadied Berry's jangling nerves sufficiently to enable her to respond with at least outward serenity when the mayor came forward smiling, and bade her, 'Come, my dear. We'll open the ball together.'

Julian danced with the mayoress, and Trish and Alan circled past them. Watching them, Berry's heart contracted. Alan's eyes were fixed on his wife's face as if, for him, she was the only person in the room, and she, looking back, seemed to have a glow about her like an invisible halo.

Berry wondered if the two knew how very lucky they were, and decided they did, and somehow the certainty seemed to make the prospect of her own future even bleaker than before.

A few minutes later, Trish confided the reason for her glowing looks when she captured Berry to come and sit at a table with them after the first few dances came to an end.

Julian was already there, talking to Alan, and Berry hung back, but Trish was insistent, and without alerting curiosity Berry could not refuse to make a foursome.

So far she had avoided dancing with Julian. When she saw him coming towards her, she managed to escape into the arms of another partner before he could get near, but she supposed wearily that her luck could not continue, and accepted the drink he brought to her with a feeling of fearful anticipation.

Answering a comment from Alan, Julian was saying genially, 'We shall all miss the campaign when it's finished. It'll leave quite a gap in our lives.'

Berry surveyed him curiously above the rim of her glass. She had not imagined that Julian would feel any gap, except the one left by Kathleen. He was totally self-sufficent. But perhaps he was only being polite.

Trish put in with a grin, 'There won't be a gap for long. Alan and I will soon find you something to do.' Relishing their attention, she went on mysteriously, 'In fact, we'll give you an extra job each. Berry can have two. She can help me to decorate the nursery.'

'The nursery?' Berry's eyes widened. 'Trish, you don't mean ...'

'I do mean. Bob rang us up from the lab when we got home this afternoon, and the tests are positive. We've both been dying to get you two on your own, to tell you. We want you to be godparents when the time comes. John, or his wife, can be the other, depending on whether it's a boy or a girl.'

Decorate a nursery. Become a godparent.

'When?' Berry asked, and Trish answered joyfully, 'Round about next Easter.'

By next Easter, if her plans worked out, Berry would be far away from Aldermouth, maybe even abroad. No distance could be too great, she felt, to place between herself and Julian but, even as her mind probed the possibilities, it rejected each one, because however many miles she journeyed, she still had to carry the leaden weight of her heart along with her.

For the moment, however, her plans had to be set to one side, as the talk centred on the coming baby. Names came to the fore, and Trish groaned, 'What a task! There are so many. In the last couple of hours, since we heard, Alan and I have been through the complete alphabet, and we haven't come up with a single one, so far.'

'We've got months to choose a name,' Alan soothed. 'Julian's got the hardest job, to find a name for the new ward. It should be finished in a matter of weeks now. Have you decided on what to call it, Julian?'

'Yes, I've chosen a name.'

'*You've* chosen a name?' Berry choked on her wine. 'You can't simply choose a name yourself, just like that. It has to be one that the whole committee agrees on.'

Julian was still doing it! Still assuming that he had the sole right to make decisions, and Berry's ire rose. This was not a medical matter, so nothing gave Julian precedence, and wrathfully she set out to dent his arrogance.

'Any name you've thought of will have to be put before the committee for a vote.' She would vote against it, she decided, and wondered with a sudden qualm if she would have the fortitude, if that name should turn out to be Kathleen.

'I've already asked the committee.'

'You didn't ask me.'

'The others agreed unanimously, so the majority vote won.'

And Julian had won, again. The glint in his eyes underlined his victory, and Berry grated, 'Am I allowed to ask what you're going to call it?'

'The Berry ward.'

'The *what*?'

'It was your idea. It should be commemorated.'

'What for?' It no longer seemed important to Berry that it should be known as her idea. She found herself wondering why it had ever seemed important.

It had been disastrous from her point of view, since it had brought her into contact with Julian in a way she could not have envisaged when she'd first thought of it, and she wanted no commemoration of something that had brought her only frustration and heartache.

'If you must use my name, why not call it the Baker ward? Surely that's more dignified than a silly nickname. Or better still, find another one.'

'There's a reason,' Julian began, but just at that moment the music started up again, and his reason was lost as Alan held out his arms to Berry, and invited gaily,

'Care to dance with a prospective father?'

Anything was better than dancing with Julian, but two circuits of the room were more than sufficient to tell Berry that her partner's mind was still back at the table with Trish.

The second time Alan stood on her toes, Berry laughingly waved away his apologies, and surrendered her claim to the rest of the dance. 'Go back to Trish and try the alphabet the other way round,' she teased, and paid the price of her generosity when Julian rose from his chair and claimed her straight from Alan's arms.

He gave her no time to make excuses. No time to plead tiredness. His arms enveloped her, and he swept her with him on to the floor.

He danced with a lithe grace that was completely at variance with Alan's performance, and Berry followed his steps with ease. She was a natural dancer, and adjusted to his firm hold upon her waist, matching her steps to his so that they moved together in perfect unison.

It was a unison that did not extend to her feelings. If she had been dancing with anyone else, it would have been bliss, but with Julian it was pure torment.

A sweet torment, that thrilled to the feel of the taut muscles rippling against her in the movement of the dance, of the crisp whiteness of his shirt-front against her cheek, and his chin brushing the top of her hair as he bent his head over her.

Was it only his chin she felt? Her eyes flew up, her feet missed a step, and she stumbled and would have fallen if he had not tightened his arms round her and held her up.

His lips lifted, triumphant from their stolen journey across her hair, and mocking the effect it had had upon her, for that had been plain for him to see. Berry's heart twisted. The music pierced her, joining in the mockery, and she was only half-aware of a voice speaking to her from another couple who danced close by.

'Did you enjoy the fireworks this evening, Miss Baker?'

It was David, the son of the fishing skipper. He danced with a lightness of foot born of the agility needed to keep his balance on the tossing deck of his father's boat.

Berry nodded and smiled automatically, and felt Julian's breath a zephyr in her ear as he murmured amusedly, 'You're not above setting off a few fireworks on your own account. Those you fired at the woman on the promenade this evening were right on target.'

Berry stiffened in his arms. 'What the woman said has got nothing to do with you.'

'I didn't say it had.'

'You didn't have to. The look on your face said quite enough.'

'What do you mean by that?' he growled. And, before she could resist his change of direction, he twirled her through a pair of open french doors, on to a wide terrace overlooking the sea.

Tubs of greenery and hanging flower-baskets hid them from the dancers in the ballroom, and Julian swung Berry to a halt underneath a spreading palm, and demanded once again, 'What do you mean by that?'

'Let me go. I want to go back in. It—it's cold out here.'

Berry tried to twist herself free from his hold. The terrace was too sheltered to be cold. It borrowed warmth from the ballroom, and her palpitating heart supplied any more that she might need.

'If you're cold, you can have my jacket across your shoulders.'

'*No!*' If Julian put his jacket across her shoulders again, her demoralisation would be complete.

As it was, with his hands holding her, pressing her close against him, and his eyes searching her upturned face, it took every bit of her strength to hold on to her wavering self-control.

'I don't want your jacket,' she refused desperately.

'I want an answer to my question. What did the look on my face say to you?'

His arms tightened round her remorselessly, his voice demanded, and she must answer him before the inferno his closeness was igniting inside her melted her resistance, and she burst into tears and confessed her love, crowning her humiliation.

It was better to die in battle than to be vanquished, and Berry fought back bravely.

'The woman only spoke half a dozen words, but your expression told me you'd drawn your own conclusions, and blamed me for them. Don't try to deny it. Your look condemned ...'

'The woman, not you. She was a spiteful, acid-tongued old harpy, and she deserved to land in court herself for her vicious gossip.'

'B-but ...' Berry stammered, completely taken aback.

'I hated her for hurting you.' Julian folded her close protectively, and punctuated his words with the lightest of kisses that came to rest like butterflies on her eyes, her lips, her chin. 'What made you think I was blaming you?'

'You blamed me for the auction. You were angry with me then. You shouted at me.'

'I was furious.'

'It wasn't my fault.'

'I know that. John told me. But at the time I couldn't help myself. I was mad with fury. With jealousy, I suppose.'

'Jealousy?' Berry echoed out of a growing sense of unreality.

'How do you imagine I felt, having to stand by and watch the woman I'm going to marry being bid for in an open auction by half the men in the hospital?'

The woman he was going to marry! Berry's mind spun. Her mouth opened to speak, but no words came, and Julian promptly closed it with his lips pressed tenderly above her own, parting their soft fullness for a long moment before Berry wrenched them away.

'You don't know what you're saying!' What he was saying was twisting a knife in her heart that made her feel as if she would die from the wound.

'I know every word I'm saying. From the moment I

first set eyes on you in the hospital chapel, I knew there could be no one else for me. I found out where you lived, and haunted the area, hoping to catch a glimpse of you.'

So that was why he had found her flat with such ease the first night he took her home! Berry's eyes were wide with the discovery as Julian confessed,

'I've longed to tell you before. I don't know how I found the strength to hold back until now.'

'You don't know anything about me. I've been married before. You heard, this afternoon . . .' Her heart pounded, but her mind presented her with cold reality, forcing her to continue doggedly, 'Your marriage was different. It was real. You can't know anything about mine.'

'I know everything, Berry. It explained a lot about you that I couldn't understand. I knew even before that awful woman spoke to you. I know the man who was your lawyer.'

'You've been checking up on me!' Swift anger flooded Berry.

'I've been doing nothing of the kind. You must believe me, Berry. It happened quite by chance.'

'Some chance!'

'It's true. The day I met Mary in America, apparently every other word I spoke was your name. Which wasn't surprising, since I never stopped thinking about you. Mary was delighted. She wrote and told Tom about it, and he recognised your name.'

'It was notorious enough locally, at the time.' Berry's voice held all the bitterness and hurt of that awful time.

'Nothing of the kind. Tom was your lawyer. Coincidence, isn't it?' He smiled at her look of startled disbelief. 'He wrote to me straight away, and warned me ...'

'To steer clear of me?'

'No, of course not. Just the opposite, in fact.' Julian pressed admonishing fingers against Berry's lips to stop her from speaking such heresy. 'Tom told me not to hurry you too fast. He said you were the sweetest creature he'd ever seen, caught up in a mesh of someone else's making, and if I tried to hurry you I might frighten you away after such a dreadful experience, and lose you altogether.'

His eyes darkened. 'I couldn't bear the prospect of losing you, so somehow I made myself hold back. But I'm not made of stone, Berry. I had to tell you that I love you. To know if you could ever bring yourself to love me.'

Gone was the self-confident, arrogant surgeon Berry thought she knew, and in his place was the real man, who bared his heart, and gave her the power to break it.

'If you'll marry me, I swear you'll never be hurt again. I'll spend the rest of my life trying to make you happy.'

He was making her happy now. Berry's heart soared like a bird in her breast, into a sky that was sunlit and beckoning. But it still held one small cloud of doubt, and its shadow drifted across her face. Julian saw it, and begged the more earnestly,

'Won't you even try? Can't you ever forget the past, the way you were hurt? Don't let it stand in the way of our happiness now, Berry, please.'

There was only one thing that might stand in the way of their happiness, and a courage she did not know she possessed drove Berry to voice it, 'Won't Kathleen come between us? When I first saw you, that day in the chapel ...'

She choked on the words, but if the cloud was ever to be lifted they had to be spoken, and when they were said, her head dropped as the tears finally spilled over.

'Look at me, Berry.'

Julian cupped her wet, white cheeks in his hands, and tipped them up to make her look at him. Her fearful eyes took in every dear, familiar feature of his face. The firm, hatchet jaw, the muscle twitching spasmodically under the skin, as she had seen it twitch that first day in the hospital chapel, under the pressure of unbearable emotion.

His voice was rough with harshly controlled feeling, but there was a new light in Julian's eyes, like twin fires buring in their green depths, and he spoke steadily, making every word count.

'Your marriage is a long time into the past. Mine is even longer. I was only a boy when I married Kathleen, and the boy I was then will always love the girl she was then. Can you understand that, Berry?'

Berry nodded dumbly, and her heart plummeted earthwards as the cloud grew darker and darker, shutting out the sunlight.

Julian went on more quietly, remembering, 'That first day you saw me in the chapel, I had just had to take a decision to switch off someone's life-support machine. Just as another surgeon, all those years ago, had to take the same decision for me. The hospital grapevine at the time said that it was my own decision. They probably blamed me for it.' His eyes devoured her face, understanding her hatred of those inevitable, gossiping tongues. 'They were wrong. But the agony was the same.

It still hurts, it always will, when I have to inflict the same suffering on someone else.'

His wide compassion agonised for someone else, while his eyes beseeched her, begging her to understand, and his voice was rough as he continued,

'The hurt for me is long into the past. I'm not a boy any more. I'm a man, and I'm offering you a man's love. The man I am now, to the woman you are now. It won't be easy, being married to a surgeon. You've seen how it can be. Missed meals. Broken appointments. But my work's a lifetime commitment. It has to be.'

Berry knew exactly what he meant. Her heart took wings again. She was committed to Julian for life, and nothing else mattered any more.

'Will you take a man's love, Berry?' he begged her. 'Will you marry me? My heart, my darling, don't refuse me. I can't face life without you.'

With a groan, he crushed her to him, and rained urgent kisses on her mouth. His arms entreated her. His lips pleaded with her. And Berry's heart soared on in bright sunlight, with not a cloud to mar the blue, giving her the courage to respond, 'If you will take a woman's love.' She raised her arms, and closed the link between them, the sure, strong link that would never be broken.

A blissful age later, her laughter mingled with that of Julian's when he murmured wickedly in her ear, 'Now you know why we can't call the new ward the Baker ward. I won't rest until you've changed your name to mine.'

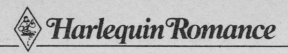 **Harlequin Romance**

## Coming Next Month

### 2941 WHIRLPOOL OF PASSION Emma Darcy
Ashley finds Cairo fascinating, and even more so the mysterious
sheikh she encounters in the casino. She's aware their attraction is
mutual, but doesn't take it seriously until he kidnaps her....

### 2942 THIS TIME ROUND Catherine George
It's all very well for Leo Seymour to want to share her life, Davina
thinks, but she can't forget that his first love married her brother
years ago. Would Davina's secret love for him be enough to sustain
their relationship?

### 2943 TO TAME A TYCOON Emma Goldrick
It isn't that Laura absolutely doesn't trust tycoon Robert Carlton;
she only wants to protect her young daughter from him. And Robert
has all his facts wrong about Laura. If there was only some way to
change their minds about each other.

### 2944 AT FIRST SIGHT Eva Rutland
From the time designer Cicely Roberts accidentally meets
psychiatrist-author Mark Dolan, her life is turned upside down.
Even problems she didn't know she had get straightened out—and
love comes to Cicely at last!

### 2945 CATCH A DREAM Celia Scott
Jess is used to rescuing her hapless cousin Kitty from trouble, but
confronting Andros Kalimantis in his lonely tower in Greece is the
toughest thing she's ever done. And Kitty hadn't warned her that
Andros is a millionaire....

### 2946 A NOT-SO-PERFECT MARRIAGE Edwina Shore
James's suspected unfaithfulness was the last straw. So Roz turned
to photography, left James to his business and made a successful
career on her own. So why should she even consider letting him
back into her life now?

Available in November wherever paperback books are sold,
or through Harlequin Reader Service:

In the U.S.
901 Fuhrmann Blvd.
P.O. Box 1397
Buffalo, N.Y. 14240-1397

In Canada
P.O. Box 603
Fort Erie, Ontario
L2A 5X3

# Take 4 best-selling love stories FREE

## Plus get a FREE surprise gift!

*Taylor House*

# by Leigh Anne Williams

Enter the lives of the Taylor women of Greensdale, Massachusetts, a town where tradition and family mean so much. A story of family, home and love in a New England village.

Don't miss the Taylor House trilogy, starting next month in Harlequin American Romance with #265 *Katherine's Dream*, in October 1988, and followed by #269 *Lydia's Hope* and #273 *Clarissa's Wish* in November and December of 1988.

### One house . . . two sisters . . . three generations

TYLRG-1